T0373521

MENAP 2089

PANTHER OPTIKONZ

authorHOUSE®

AuthorHouse™
1663 Liberty Drive
Bloomington, IN 47403
www.authorhouse.com
Phone: 833-262-8899

Published by AuthorHouse 01/21/2021

ISBN: 978-1-6655-1475-0 (sc)
ISBN: 978-1-6655-1474-3 (e)

Print information available on the last page.

CHAPTER 1

Reflections of sunlight has just flickered off a cab driving by and shone across the many oknos of the AirBus-57821 heading towards Ellsworth and Crescent streets. Many of the lewdies aboard this Airbus would at some point transfer to the Hyperloop train on their way to District 1. The Merchant section in District 1 had just opened up and many recent graduates from District 7 were hopeful in gaining employment. District 7 was the poorest district and many lewdies starved to death or were usually drug addicted. Although there were some parishes in each district that was better to-do than others, most usual disparities between the districts were always pointed at the fault of the Cornucopia Capitol. The Cornucopia Capitol was shaped like a big metal like horn, which stood upside down. Some people would refer to it as "that ugly water discus hotel." It sat erected from its stem within the high level ocean just west off the coast of the city of Menap. The city of Menap 2089 previously was San Francisco more than seventy-five years ago and before the apocalyptic war brought on by the forces against The Order. District 1 is the biggest nation in Menap and it also serves as the most affluent next to the Capitol. The Capitol is the central point of government and rules over the seven districts where each district is separated as its own nation-state. The lower a person's district was in rank, the more special permission was required in order to leave and visit or work in another district. Otherwise it was illegal and a lewdy was sure to be captured and dealt with by the millicent. Those who lived in Districts 1 through 4 were free city dwellers and could go about as they pleased.

The loud honking of a horn was shrill and demanding as it stirred an old drunken man sitting near a stopped cab as two men entered it. He was a smelly old man, most likely homeless. He could often be seen singing loud and drinking and yelling vile epithets to passersby. "One thing I could never stand about Menap is to viddy a filthy, dirty old pyahnitsa, howling away at the filthy songs of his fathers and going blerp, blerp in between as it might be a filthy old orchestra in his stinking rotten guttiwutts. I could never stand to viddy anyone like that, whatever his age might be, but more especially when he was real starry like this one here," said the cab driver who was behind the wheel of an ETV touchscreen mobile pod. With a commuter's boredom he glanced behind at his two passengers who weren't listening. The fat man's blunt litso contrasted with his expensive suit and cream shirt. The *mob* always alternated the drivers and their passengers because no one ever knew who to trust in this business. Cars were getting blown up mysteriously recently. There was the conservatively dressed Audubon Kissel, often spoke affectionately of his home life in District 1 and of his wife, his children, his connections to the Capitol. His partner next to him was the smiling Hector 'The Knight Rider" Savarese. He liked the ponies and devotchkas and liked to exchange in vulgar activity as often as time would allow. The corpulent Audubon and his droog Hector didn't care what avenues or streets were used just as long as they got *up there* and back in the shortest possible time to do business. The fat man barely grunted any complaint this time as he patiently waited out the ride. Hector on the contrary was always quite bitchy.

The dying sun shredded through the trees onto the elderly who sat as though in despair and watched the molodoy as they goolied by in their shorts and jumpers, carrying video call screens. Several children hurriedly grabbed onto monkey bars and played hard as they soared on swings before the sun would go down in just a few hours. The road twisted and turned around Android Park as the two men sat in the rear of the cab, anxiously waiting to arrive in the T-1 parish, which was situated in District 5.

Big-busted Negresses stared broodingly down from the oknos of the crippled buildings, like benign goddesses in cunning towers watching the crowded, agitated street below them. Hector rolled his okno down only to hear radios spewing war threats, raucous gangster music and children cursing about.

"Who teaches them such language?" remarked the fifty-two winters Hector; at this old his aging white litso grimaced at the children's lithe onyx bodies glistening in the brilliant sunlight. In the slow moving traffic they passed the flaring neon lit liquor stores, movie houses and restaurants. Music blared from bars and record shops, a mélange of staccato beats that were picked up by the hipsters lounging along the curb eyeing the high-assed girls going seductively by. The Raven Mockers worked their trade from second-story perches and the married couples okno-shopped below in the *pimps up and whores down* jewelry and clothing stores. The Red Vic Movie House was again double-featuring the famous films *Ataska* and *Poked Doll* and Audubon noticed that one of the oknos of his secret lewdy was missing.

Then an inconspicuous car turned into a side block and came silently to a stop. Several molodoy were gathered under a street lamp, harmonizing an imitation of the latest rock-and-roll hit. A few domy's down a mother called out, "Capricornica, Capricornica" impatiently from an upper-floor okno. "Don't you hear what I say, come up here now!" A drunken bratchny pulls up a cancer from a carman while moving as if he had bellied to a bar far too long after work and was now on his way home to a tongue-lashing wife. This was a block less congested than most, three-story doms sitting back from the street, their stoops leading to second-floor vestibules still showing semblances of once-proud turn-of-the-century elegance.

Audubon and his droog Hector get out of the cab as they have finally reached their destination. The fat man's dark glazzies and leathery litso had now lost some of the boredom. Audubon scanned the street briefly to viddy if anyone was on his track as he just paid the faire.

"The damn millicent was on my dook the last time," says the stout Audubon.

"Well be careful, act cool and keep your rookers down. Don't be so skorry," insisted the grouchy Hector who stood much taller and thinner.

"Well you're the one that's always bitching!" screamed Aubudon.

"Did you sloosh recently about the missing 1933 Gold Double Eagle coin, somebody at the Lodge replaced it with a counterfeit," Hector rebutted and by this time Aubudon slipped over an oily area in the walkway because he wasn't paying attention and falls into some bushes.

"Watch the drencrom...you hear...I said watch the shit!" blurted Hector. Hector truly was a mean spirited person as he doesn't even offer to assist Audubon up to his nogas again. Poor Audubon was so nervous and paranoid all the time. Meanwhile Hector takes offense at all this newfound commotion because he feels that Audubon is up to something which furthers his suspiciousness about the missing Golden Eagle coin that the *big boss* wants and takes blame to everyone in The Lodge.

"Well then you fucking carry the valise asshole.....and what coin are you talking about anyway!" Audubon asked.

"You mean you don't know?"

"No I don't know, what is there to know?" Audubon complained.

Both men were barely conscious of the curiosity and hostile stares from the people sitting on the darkened stoops around them; they meant nothing, they scarcely saw them, for they were the normal still-life. Audubon carried the large valise and followed Hector up the front stairs to the second-floor vestibule of the domy. They didn't stop to smot for a name or ring a bell but pushed through the unlocked door as if they had done this before. Both chellovecks decided to keep their conversations to a minimum until they got to a safer place. A dim gray light from the rear halls washed across them through the spokes of the banister as they climbed the stairs to the top floor. They moved along the dark hall, almost groping, to another section of the domy. The hardened litso of a worried Negro-Veck man, Isaac Payne, met them at the front of a door as the chelloveck's footsteps seemed muted for some odd reason.

Led by Isaac, the two men entered a dingy room that reeked of dank smoke. Its shades were drawn and an old-fashioned cloth-shaded lamp hung low from the ceiling, throwing its yellowish glow onto a table, which was completely cleared except for a very large amount of pretty polly piled loosely into bundles. Some coins dropped to the floor. Two well-dressed Negro-Vecks standing beside the table both just nodded a greeting. The one who had let them in relocked the door and casually leaned against it. The sitting Audubon passed the large valise to another droog named Eddie Many Holes in order to be laid onto the table where it was opened without any hesitation. Eddie took a small notebook from his inside carman and began to write down detail of everything. Hector stood back to blend in, only he was the other lone White dude—for now besides his partner Audubon at least—everyone else was Negro-Veck or a Mongoloid to Indian.

No time could be wasted on formalities. The Anglo-Veck man, sweat now running freely down his litso, stopped on occasion to wipe his brow. He began to write down jots of figures on a piece of paper, adjusting his otchkies during the process. The three men, holding their cancer sticks loosely from their goobers, became completely engrossed in the tabulations. The ancient lamp above their gullivers, which helped to distort their litsos with its harsh light, grew to be too much and Eddie stepped over into another direction with less light as Isaac got up and disappeared to a backroom. The squawk from a Cuckoo Clock positioned just above a fireplace, shows it had struck one full hour and the room had become completely silent except for the sorting of the stolen cutter.

"Are you droogs ready to viddy pink elephants flying in the sky?" asked Isaac to everyone as he walked in the center of the room while carrying a trey full of tasses.

"The Korova Spacebar sold milk-plus, milk plus vellocet or synthemesc or drencrom, can't remember, but this will sharpen you up and make you ready for a bit of the old ultraviolence!" shouted Isaac as he goolied back with several tasses.

"Welly, welly, welly, well to what do I owe you of the extreme pleasure of the surprising visit?" asked Gary Overdrawn trying to engage further in the subject of ultraviolence.

But then odd zvooks by the front door were heard first by one of the men at the table. Gary Overdrawn's brow furrowed, his glazzies flicked up, he darted a glance at the door and then relaxed. It was just innocuous footsteps, no need to worry. Some sookas were expected soon for the old lubbilubbing later, maybe they were arriving early. However, the organization of all true droogs emulated the banking corporations that, when transferring large sums, used the busy time of day, the crowded streets and a limited number of guards. Except for the fact that this was a crast of the green papered pretty polly and must always be guarded, the pickup of the weekly take was carried on against an active background. This location was perfect because it was accustomed to a flurry of prestoopniks riding up in touring cars and emptying hoods onto a street to scare a neighborhood with intimidating scowls and bulging pooshkas under form-fitting platties.

A knock erupted at the door. Each chelloveck tensed, his guttiwutts knotting. Each smotted quickly, nervously about and stood for what seemed an incredibly long minute. Then the knock came again; just as insistent. The Negro-Vecks at the door peered anxiously from the shadows at the two White men chellovecks. One began to move in closer with a pooshka in one hand.

"Viddy who it is."

The Black man's goloss cut through the tension of the room with a hardness that belied his appearance. Several droogs pulled their pooshkas out as well and aimed for the door as Audubon opened the door slowly. Peering out, he smotted through the small opening and his body froze for a moment. Then slowly he turned back inside. His litso, shadowed, was controlled, but his tenseness was evident from his hushed, perplexed goloss.

"IT'S THREE SOOKAS!"

The words bounced off like an electrical charge. Suddenly the droogs retreated their pooshkas and grew a pan-handle as the three sexy sookas carefully goolied in. It was obvious that these women had just come from the **Afropunk Decompression Party** because of the sparkle and fanciness in their *platties*. One woman had huge groodies up top and her cleavage was massive.

"I'd say its right, right time we perform the old in-out, in-out on this here devotchka." Leroy Lovelace said as he moved in on the efforts of lubbilubbing towards one of the girls. Isaac begins to openly massage his yarblockos and edges towards the ladies direction. His rooker rubs violently against her sharries with a heavy grasp and intent to go much further. Everything seems so rushed and brash, but the damas are used to this. They know they are sookas working hard for the cutter and wouldn't even know a better role in life to choose anyhow.

"Can you spare some cutter, me brothers?" asked one of the girls, her lips red and wet and hardly recognizable with all her make-up and drooginess.

"And who are you?" A brother shouted.

"Why I am Grenique John Horse Goddess of the Floating Fortresses."

"There're not sookas!" screamed Gary Overdrawn. His words burst more in astonishment than in warning. But it was too late. The hand that was partially hidden behind Yogita's platty was armed with an ultra-pooshka and out she brought it in plain view.

"Over to the okno all of you!" Yogita and her girls all pulled out their semi-ultra pooshkas as well and threatened the droogs. The men motioned away from the table and the cutter. Sheila twists Leroy's rooker and he backs off.

"Now, nice and slow you throw your pooshkas onto the floor!" Sheila demanded while pointing the gun at them.

A flurry of weapons tolchocked the floor as the men disarmed themselves. Grenique and Sheila help each other open a black trash bag, while Yogita shoves the loads of green pretty polly into it. Gray smoke bombs from the cancer sticks of the chellovecks fill the room.

It was the mistake the Negro-Vecks who had allowed them in was waiting for. Leroy bent quickly, silently. He makes a lip-trump followed by a dog howl, followed by two fingers pronged into the air, followed by a clowny guffaw. Grenique picks up what looks to be a pool stick and slams it smartly on Leroy's legs. He screeches out in pain from the blow.

"What you go and do that for!" Leroy screams at Grenique.

"For being a bastard with no manners and not a dook of an idea on how to comport yourself public wise, O my Brother." Grenique retorts.

"I don't like what you have done, and I am not your brother no more and wouldn't want to be." Leroy gasps.

"Watch that; do watch that Negro-Veck, if to continue · to be one of the living as thou dost wish." Grenique snarled.

Leroy's fingers had already curled around the grip of Sheila's pooshka when the bogus baboochka turned back. Eddie and Gary bumped into each other as neither one knew which way to go. Gary's move went toward the gunner, for his attention was riveted upon the Octagonic Sten-gun rising in Grenique's rookers. Audubon's goloss was high-pitched, as if only he knew what was about to happen next.

"No, no, don't!"

The bellowed screech of warning was lost in the explosion of sounds from Grenique's Octagonic Sten-gun and the girls' pooshkas. The bullets tore into several droogs, spinning them and driving them back against the wall and front oknos. A plott hung, momentarily welded to the partition, its glazzies wide open in disbelief; and then slowly, grotesquely it slid to the floor. The zvook of glass from the shattered oknos tinkled on the cement of the street below.

The girls stood motionless, their ookos still pounding

from the now-quiet Octagonic Sten-gun while a thin trail of vapor waved up past their litsos from its heated nozzle. In front of Sheila, a nogas twitched, a rooker moved and from the wall a beseeching cry of repentance: "Jesus, oh Jesus, Mary …." and then a terrible silence. The room tilted and spun around Eddie Many Holes and he could feel the nausea rising from the depths of his stomach, through his chest and into his gorlo. He turned from the carnage and the sight that greeted him restored his rassoodock to sharp awareness. His droog Hector was doubled over, one hand holding the table for support, belching vomit onto the overturned valise. Audubon moved swiftly across the room, grabbed the rooker of his partner Hector and shook it violently. "Goddammit, man, you don't crap out on me now. Not now!" The goloss of the stout man guttered with distortion as he fought back his own terror, his own sickness.

"Doobidoob... a bit tired maybe, everybody is. A long night for growing devotchkas... best not to say more. Bedways is right ways now, so best we go homeways and get a bit of spatchka. Right, right!" said Grenique out of breath and yanking the draw-cords closed on the bag. She jammed it up under her arm and turned to the door leaving with the girls. They turned at the end of the hall and pounded down the flight of steps. They were halfway down when the outer door was pushed open and two millicents filled the vestibule entrance, their ultra-pooshkas drawn. The shallow grayness of the outside street lamp came through the door, partially silhouetting the devotchkas plotts which aided in blending them into barriers to escape.

"Well hey there," said the rozz. There was a catch of caution in the rozzer's goloss as he squinted quizzically up at what appeared to be Black sookas coming from shopping at the Tacky Store. But to their surprise, Grenique retrieves her Octagonic Sten-gun. Again there was a deafening staccato of bursting sounds and the two rozzers fell as though a child had moved a heavy hand, downing tin soldiers. The bullets had chopped across their litsos, leaving them in their twisted dead positions with incredulous blood-soaked stares.

In the vestibule Sheila slipped going over one rozz, who had been blown back through the door. His nogas went across, forcing a gasp of air from the dying man's lungs.

The devotchkas tolchocked the sidewalk in a rush of panic. A Durango-95 blaring doobidoob from out the speakers of a radio with its headlight noticeably busted out, came up fast, cutting in toward the curb and just missing the empty *prowl* car. The driver, un-recognizable, slowed barely enough to receive the shaikas as they frantically tore open the doors and piled in. The gears shifted and the auto-tron took the corner on skidding, screeching tires, leaving the street and the surrounding area in a state of shock. But no lewdy would dare come forth govoreeting with anyone what they'd just viddied.

CHAPTER 2

Piercing sirens wailed along CC-100 and MS-007 streets, flaring up over Twenty Four Arch Android and C-1000 streets. The angry shrieks rose, wave upon wave, meeting responding shrieks from CS-101 and DH-006 Blvd until all of the area seemed saturated with the sounds.

The wall of people in District 7 parted as the siren growled just enough to clear a path to the wooden barricades which held the curious back. The rozz by the blockade pulled part of it aside and waved detectives through. They eased the car into the block, which now vibrated with a perverse excitement. They could feel it as they stepped into the street and threaded their way between the haphazardly parked patrol pods and unmarked detectives' vehicles with millicent radio frequencies rolling out static monotones. The detectives goolied past the vehicles of broadcasters and newspapermen. The rolling millicent lab was next to the curb.

The tenement telegraph had sent its message and the teeming multitudes had responded. They passed against the roped-off areas in front of the domy and every okno on the block was darkened by plotts that leaned precariously from the ledges. People stood on the roofs and hoods of futuristic looking automobiles, caught in the long splashes of scarlet mixed with amber from the flashing lights atop the patrol pods, and hundreds more people had gathered at the intersections. The street possessed a morbid carnival air that forced the two detectives to quicken their pace up the glass-littered stoop. The okno panels were blown out of the doors and the vestibule was pockmarked with bullets. The rozz assigned to the death watch glanced dolefully at them. A blood-soaked shoe lay in the corner and the plotts had been pulled from the entrance and placed along the inner wall. A twisted silver trouser leg stuck out from one of the canvas covers. The detectives continued up the stairs. At the landing they had to squeeze past civilian-clad inspectors and other detectives, who stood outside the room nodding and talking in the hushed tones one would use at a wake.

Inside, the harsh flash floods by photographers reflected off the gold-braided hats and shiny buttons of grim-faced millicent chiefs. Lab chelloveks were dusting the table and the walls, and taking the identification prints of the dead who lay within chalked outlines. Shadows of profiles and full figures jumped along the walls as the artificial brightness transformed the room into an abstract black-on-white world.

"Fuck, this is going to be some nochy," a molodoy detective said, easing past two chellovecks who had just come in.

"Any leads yet?" one of them asked.

The molodoy detective stopped, seemed about to say

something, then shrugged and stepped past them, his goloss coming back softly over his pletcho. "You find out," he said, and disappeared into the hall.

The taller of the two detectives, Patrick Magee was a Negro-Veck, his lean, athletic frame enhancing his conservative dark tropical suit. His high cheekbones and aquiline nose gave him almost the look of a Native American or an "NA-Veck", but the soft brown glazzies and the heavy lips underlined the African heritage proclaimed by his amber-brown skin. He was a Black man. Simple.

His partner Phillip Stoner, white and ruddy-faced, nudged him. "Come on," he said in a whisper.

The two of them goolied over to the department captain, who stood in civilian platties in the center of the room, conversing with a dignified-looking dedoochka. They stopped just short of overhearing, but in a position to be seen, and waited. The Anglo-Veck detective had a square jaw, pugnacious nose and wore deep narrow glazzies on an Irish litso that supposedly spelled "rookie rozz." He was taller than average, but his stocky, muscular frame shortened his appearance. His platties had a slightly rumpled, uncared-for look.

The dedoochka talking to the captain shook his gulliver to signal the end of the official conversation and, picking up the unmistakable black leather bag of a medical examiner, goolied past the detectives. They held their distance a moment longer as Captain Warren Clarke looked broodingly at the crowded, active room. He seemed relatively molodoy, but as they goolied up to him the lines around his glazzies magnified through the deep contours around his rot and shiyah.

"I would have messeled by now that thou would still be on the leave of bolnoy, Phillip. Is everything dobby?" Clarke spoke to the Anglo-Veck detective in a tired tone that somehow still carried genuine concern.

Phillip Stoner stared at him before answering, trying to read another meaning into the question, but he found none in the deep gray glazzies. "I got a clean bill of health from the surgeon's office this morning." He paused, then added reassuringly, "everything's all right, Captain. I'm fine."

They held the stare for a couple of seconds. "Real horrorshow," Clarke said finally. "I'm going to need every chelloveck on the squad." His gaze drifted toward the front of the room and settled on the covered plotts laying in front of the bullet-pitted wall and broken oknos. "We got a hell of a mess on our hands, Phillip. Four *got it* up here and you saw what was left in the hall."

"What about witnesses, Captain?" the molodoy detective asked. "Are there any lewdies we can start to work from?" His articulation was sharp.

Clarke turned to him. His litso hardened and the gray glazzies came through the horn-rimmed otchkies. "Sure," he said. "All that shooting and the front oknos lying out in the street, I would say maybe fifty lewdies got some kind of a smot at who did this. Enough witnesses to where we could have a good composite, but we can't get any of them to come forward. We've already checked the street and talked to the lewdies in the adjoining buildings, but nobody's viddied a thing." He didn't try to conceal the contempt he felt for the neighborhood. "Because these lewdies don't want to know from nothing. They're rozz haters and if a couple of rozzers got killed tonight, fine, that's just fine. It's two less they have to vred."

The room had fallen silent and the chellovecks watched as the death detail moved in. The ambulance attendants, with their stretchers and canvas bags, pulled off the hasty coverings the rozzers had thrown over the plotts and started bundling the dead towards the waiting death vans for the ride town-down to the cold slabs of the morgue. They turned a twisted plott onto its back, the black litso now ashen in a strangely peaceful repose as if death brought the beautiful spatchka. Stoner took a quick glance at Clarke, then back to another litso—another Negro-Veck—but this litso held the horrorshow of the killing. His left rooker had the tattoo marked Basquiat's Boys. The open glazzies stared blindly, the goobers were parted wide, and Stoner could almost sloosh the creech that had rolled out of the purple rot.

When the last weaving stretcher had passed him, Stoner said, "They're Basquiat's boys." His goloss was flat and controlled, but the surprise came through as he realized how bolshy this shooting was, the ramifications it could have, and now he knew why Warren Clarke seemed tired and old and so deeply concerned.

"Professionals," added Stoner's partner Patrick Magee. His glazzies went across the room letting the words sink in. "This thing had to be cased too well to have amateurs behind it. But they must have been shitting in their pants pulling it off." Magee motioned toward the caked and drying vomit lying across the overturned suitcase. "It looks like Basquiat was turning over the weekly take." The goloss droned on in the city accent that seemed so colloquially appropriate to Menap rozzers. "Most gang members are usually careful about their pickup, but I guess they never thought they'd be tolchocked up here, so their guard must have been down. They didn't seem to put up a fight; we don't know if they were in any sick plan to go or if the machine-gunner panicked. But it seems somebody knew somebody, or they recognized it too late that whoever the person they think they might have known was out to turn on them."

Magee looked at the shades hanging shredded and torn at the oknos, the pools of blood on the floor coagulating to brown smears, and he remembered the plotts being packed onto stretchers. He thought of the savage violence that must have been behind the gun. Panic or not, he knew it took a cold calculation to premeditate a crime such as this, a coldness that sent a chill across his imagination. "Well they sure didn't take any chances on missing that's for sure." Stoner said, walking up to examine the okno closer.

"How could they with the arsenal they were carrying?" Magee said as he turned back to face him. "And that partially explains why the two rozzers downstairs didn't get any shots off." The captain spoke slowly, re-examining his first impressions more analytically now as if he were using them as a sounding board. "It's one of those unfortunate situations of being at the wrong place at the wrong time." He paused, the lights in the room reflecting off his otchkies; behind them his glazzies seemed to be searching for clues. "I just can't seem to understand. Anyone in my command when they seen that gun would have at least dropped them where they stood or at least got some kind of shot off." His words trailed off and he shrugged into silence, but his words hung in the seething heat of the room, chafing in the stilled cancer smoke above their gullivers like a neon light one could viddy flickering through night fog.

There were inspectors, deputy inspectors and lieutenants from various Menap private investigations agencies all congregated together on the scene. The commissioner and his chief inspector made their customary appearance, mouthed off their clichés at one another and disappeared. But the press was aware that Clarke was the department captain, so they went for him. They stuck their radio mics and television cameras into his litso; the rozzers stood on the side as though not wanting to get involved but stayed close enough to hear what he was going to say to reporters, who recorded and quoted with quick scribbled notes.

Soon after the throng had thinned out, the millicent photographers had doused their floods and were packing their gear. Several millicents lingered still, talking amongst themselves, their presence lending authority. But it was Clarke's department, his command, and he would handle the details. Only the laboratory people were still working in the painstakingly deliberate movements of their trade.

"Captain." The young rozzer's goloss was edged with an urgency that pulled Clarke around. "Yeah?" The demeanor of command returned. "Yeah, what is it?"

"A call came over the screen for you, sir. They picked up a man who rents this domy and he is being questioned at the department."

"Well good, that's real horrorshow like," said Clarke. "Tell them I'll be right over." He turned back to the detectives, tiredness still hanging over his litso, but he had pushed the perplexities to the back of his rassoodock because the tedious task of tracking down leads had begun. "I want you two to go over to the emergency ward of Menap General Hospital; one of Basquiat's droogs is still alive. How in the hell he ever survived this is to my wildest imagination. I want you to try and get as much information out of him as you possibly can before he kicks the bucket. I got every man on the squad working tonight and I told them what I am telling you two." His goloss lowered, not wishing to be overheard. "By tomorrow morning I want to have a report that can be put together for a lot of questioning from town-down. I want everything—quotes, details, everything and anything that's pertinent to this case." They both stood motionless; the order seemed too general, so they waited a moment longer for specifics and then realized they were being given initiative to move as they saw fit. They nodded confirmation, turned away and were at the door when the captain's goloss stopped them in their tracks. "Magee." There was no command in the tone. The Negro-Veck detective walked slowly back, his Anglo-Veck partner waited at the door.

"Patrick." Clarke hesitated as if he had something difficult to say. His glazzies held with Magee's for a few seconds, and then broke away uncomfortably. "Fagged I am a bit, so I'm throwing the papers in, Patrick."

"What?" Magee's flushed, brown glazz-balled face showed its sudden concern. "I figured you'd go all the way for a full forty summers at least."

"Bloody hell," Clarke said flatly. "I can't stand this cal no more; the filthy lewdies are always having a filly on my yarblockos. It's no world for any old man any longer."

"Clarke, the department is in a heap of trouble if you're

type is no longer needed. You can't retire now." Magee added. The captain's goobers moved in a malenky bit like an imperceptible smile that seemed to say thank you.

"Well if I seem tolchocked upon an edge, now you know why," Clarke said softly. "It took me quite a while to decide to pack it in." There was wistfulness in him that made Magee want to grasp his hand and wish him luck and tell him that he had made the right decision. But in this busy room with its stink of death it would have been fraternization of the worst kind. There will be a testimonial and he will be there to sing the cheers with the others across the table full of scotch and pitchers of beer and that will be the right and proper way to retire from the department once and for all.

"If this is going to be your windup," Magee said quietly, "then we're going to miss you, Clarke."

"This is the last one, Patrick, I guarantee you that. That's why I want everything done just right. I"—again he groped for the right words—"I guess I want to leave as a person who was known as an enforcer. They say the last one you work on is the one you remember." The captain's glazzies searched about the room as he assured himself he was not being overheard. His goloss became hoarse, almost a whisper. "So I'm going to handle this as it should be done. I'm going to bug a lot of bratchnies who need to be bothered, because this is going to be fillied the old way for a change. That's why I am taking the leash off you and every chelloveck in the department."

A gloopy grin started to cross Patrick Magee's litso as he caught the permeating excitement of the words. He knew the repercussions it could create, and if it was to be a strong exit he was grateful to be a spear carrier in such a final act. "What are your theories, Clarke?" Magee was surprised by the worry in his own goloss. "I think this was a local affair." The natural gruffness came back into the captain's tone; his moment of disclosure was past. "This was no hit or miss; it had to be thought out carefully, planned."

The captain's glazzies widened behind the otchkies as if in some kind of begrudging tribute. "It took a lot of balls to pull this off, but more than that, it took some inside knowledge. Maybe Basquiat's got some insurgents on his rookers." He shrugged, "I don't know, but it's still something to think about."

A paunchy, aging rozz standing with an assistant inspector was clearly impatient to give some kind of parting instructions to Clarke. He signaled that he wanted to speak to him. "If you don't get anything at the hospital I want you and your partner to stay in the streets and filly it by ear, yea." The two detectives took a step toward their superior, and then looked at each other for a moment, then Magee nodded, acknowledging the authority he was being given.

CHAPTER 3

The black steeled fence encompassed in brick ran the length of this spacious PH-3000 Mansion. It was a modern Zen House masterpiece which retained its architectural integrity from one of Menap's most prestigious locations in District 2. Set behind gates it was a winding maze of sculptural granite and glass, the granite façade and knoll top setting added to the mansion's mystique and privacy. A Black man had parked his shiny black Cambiocorsa discreetly on the quiet street and goolied up the windy driveway. His footsteps seemed a paradox in the evening heat. He had gotten the call from one of Audubon's boys and quickly driven across to this high tech designed house with its cinemascope view of the bay. He had wondered about the call and thought maybe the dedoochka was finally dying and The Family was probably being summoned to pay its last respects. But no extra cars were parked in the driveway or street and there were only a couple of lights on in the domy. The conspicuous man pressed a button and the chimes fillied their subdued chord behind the heavy oaken door. There was a wait and then the knob turned once, twice and the door flung open. The man stares down at the wide-eyed child who has just opened the door. But just as the man was about to ask a question, a stout baboochka appeared in the blue uniform of a domestic person, most likely the help.

"Junior." Her wimpy goloss was barely audible and she would have yelled at him if it had not been for some odd stranger staring at her from the door. "You no supposed to open the door. You grandfather tell you, I tell you!"

But the malchick ignored her. His large dark glazzies had already begun their search of the stranger in the doorway. Her starched uniform crinkled as she pulled the malchick's rooker from off the knob while looking hard at the stranger in the doorway. A perceptible aura of disquiet about him that seemed to manifest itself in his deep-set hazel glazzies forced a wary respect in her tone of inquiry.

"How can I help you, sir?"

"Why I have an appointment with Mr. Luciano Pavarotti." His goloss was rasp, "you can tell him Lord Perrineau is here."

She stared at him for quite some time, trying to decide what business led the stranger to her employer. Then her glazzies dropped as she recalled the many stories of rumored enterprises based on illegitimate business. But she didn't want to believe any of it. Mr. Pavarotti was a kind and honest veck. The small malchick broke away from her grip and started down the wide chandeliered hallway.

"Grandpa, Grandpa," he called, then opened a door and disappeared. The servant baboochka sighed in exasperation and motioned the stranger to enter, closing the door behind them. Lord Perrineau's glazzies took in the monstrous crystal chandelier, the ornate pearly white staircase leading to the upper floor and the paintings along the wall. The lord removed his shlapa and waited patiently. His tight plott in the dark Byard suit was trim and cared for.

The baboochka had followed the path of the malchick down the long carpeted foyer and gone into a room near the foot of the stairs. She emerged a moment later. "Okay, Mr. Pavarotti he wanna see you now."

Lord Perrineau was about to pass her. "Mister, you no stay too long, yea?" She said it quietly with a touch of pleading in her voice. "Mr. Pavarotti he no feel too horrorshow and…" Lord Perrineau's impassive stare cut her words short. She lowered her gulliver and backed off, embarrassed. As Lord Perrineau entered the door, he could hear the malchick laughing and govoreeting with some dedoochka as he was smecking away and not caring about the wicked world one bit. Then the color on the wall stereo changed and blinked green as fresh new sounds of music came on. Instantly the old man Pavarotti came with a burst of warbling to the doobidoob's theme. Lord Perrineau passes a mural of nagoy chelloveks and cheenas in the hall as doobidoob fillies the corridor.

"Come along now and be seated, Lord Perrineau has arrived." The dedoochka's hoarse goloss filled the study as Lord Perrineau entered through, but his appearance came as a shock. The little boy, sitting on the rooker of the chair as he cuddled next to his grandfather, became silent again. "To what do I owe you this supreme pleasure, sir?" Pavarotti said. But the old man was distracted as the young boy became razdrazzed at the stranger being in the room; he wanted to continue the impromptu romp. But the old man ended it.

"Okay, Junior!" He patted his grandson gently on the nogas. "You go with Elena and get your bath now." The malchick went reluctantly. He looked back at the old man, who smiled paternally, as Elena took the malchick's rooker firmly and quietly shut the door.

"Please have a seat, do allow me to fix you a firegold." The dedoochka offered.

"Doobidoob." Said the lord. He watched as the old man tried at best to conceal an illness. It was obvious the old man was bolnoy from the way he reached about in pain and agony and from his von too.

"So how do you truly feel, Mr. Pavarotti?" The lord's tone was unsympathetic but the words were respectively correct.

"Hah!" Mr. Pavarotti waved his rookers in the air with much disdain and dismissal. Lord Perrineau thought not to continue. He hadn't seen the gray haired patriarch for some time. The word had filtered down that the old veck was very ill and possibly going to kick the bucket; Lord Perrineau had discounted the rumor as wishful talk of the ambitious that were after something for themselves. But it was mainly in the glazzies which told the story, red-rimmed, tired and now too bolshy for his own gulliver.

"Everybody gets bolshy, huh; it's just my turn now. Stop worrying about it!" Pavarotti grumbled as he petted a Siamese cat.

"How baddiwad is it?" Lord Perrineau asked with consternation.

Pavarotti picked up his firegold, lights catching in the vermillion liquid as he twisted the glass slowly in his rooker. "They cut me open, take some cal out and sew me up again.

Now I viddy and wait for what happens, ya pony this."
Pavarotti sounds irritated, like he has been explaining this
over and over again. "It's a shit hole, but most of the time
I feel okay."

Lord Perrineau wanted to assure Pavarotti that he would
be real horrorshow soon, but he could see death in the
dedoochka's glazzies and litso.

"Its time you wonder where it goes. I remember when
you were just a kid; I was moving up and you were just
coming in." A wisp of melancholic smile touched the tired
litso. "You were just a malenky bit then, a lousy punk
malchick. But you did all right; you built a horrorshow of a
reputation for yourself, Lord Perrineau, with The Family. I
get the dobby reports about you all the time."

Lord Perrineau felt a certain gratification at the words
being put to him by this ranking patrician, but he didn't
know which direction the boss was taking the newspeak.
He averted his glazzies and remained silent. Pavarotti's
smile disappeared and he stared at the younger man as if
ascertaining his future value.

"So I guess you want to move up a malenky bit higher,
huh, Lord Perrineau?"

The young lord looked up quickly, found the dedoochka's
glazzies boring into him. "I never mentioned a stinking
thing about it!" the lord seemed annoyed about something.

"You don't have to; ambition is written all over you.
You're wearing three-hundred-dollar suits and expensive
shoes and I bet your shirts are made to order. You got style,
Lord Perrineau. You're a couple cuts above the average
brother that I got working for me and somehow you got
lost in the shuffle, huh?"

Lord Perrineau watched the old don rise with a noticeable effort. The emaciated plott labored as he goolied toward the gigantic painting on the wall. It was the painting of a Neteru Dragon and the many Harpies and Amanthra demons surrounding it. In a distance the lights flickered like tiny jewels in Menap's skyline and there was a dull, aggressive drone from a private jet whisking by for altitude. All at once it seemed like shooms of war, protesting and chanting as the Fighting Falcons flew by and the lewdies outside creeched at them. But Lord Perrineau never heard a zvook, for his rassoodock was too full of this enigmatic, almost threatening dedoochka. Pavarotti of course wanted it this way. He wanted Lord Perrineau's sleek hardness to squirm; he wanted to remind him that he could have him dead within a couple of hours after he left the house if he gave the order. That he controlled the destinies of shylocks, pimps, whores, pushers, bookkeepers, labor unionists, extortionists and executioners. There was lots of the pretty polly that Pavarotti controlled and his price was of the higher price, the most lucrative, with gang money to pour into the takeover of legitimate banking, investment and real estate firms. The dedoochka supervised control over recordings, jukeboxes, vending machines and big bagged securities; but now the sonofabitch was about to finally kick the bucket and for the first time he knew what fear really felt like. Pavarotti was on the national commission, maybe the biggest one of them all, and some gloopy bratchny of a surgeon cut him open, sewed him up, then sent him home, telling him he had maybe a fortnite to live. He could feel the bitter rage swelling up in his emaciated body. He, who had put the key working fix on union and business executives, elected officials and the indispensable millicents, was going to die. He had to smash out against the tomb that was closing about him, to prove to himself that he could still make his world crawl at his nogas. He turned and looked at Lord Perrineau.

"I think tonight I give you a big opportunity." The gray head nodded slowly. "Yeah, maybe after tonight I move you up from behind the shit to some kind of a piece of the shit action up front. You like that, Perrineau? Hey, I don't have to ask, huh?"

Perrineau laughs at him as he smots directly at the old veck's litso and rookers which were all mappy from being so aged. The lord takes another sip of his firegold. The liquid continues stinging from his goobers at the prick of the taste. His gulliver swings a malenky bit back and forth from the power of the liquor that is now rushing through the veins of his plot. First up, then down again like.

"I can see it in your spacey litso," Pavarotti continues, "the trouble with you, you're too horrorshow in doing your job. I farm you out of contracts all over the Districts; the other families they want to use your talents all the time. But I become blind; I keep you as nothing more than a special soldier in my regime."

The lord sat perfectly quiet near the bamboo throw of the sofa as he listened to the constant jabbering of the old man. There was a botanical framed table lamp set aside up top of a wooden console table where hors'doevres were neatly spaced apart. Perrineau helped himself to a few feeling that if he ate it might ease some of the wooziness.

The old man began to come under suspicion by all the sudden offers. Perrineau understood that if a prize was to be had in some way, in the end it had to be paid for just as the old man always got his pound of flesh in return. Still, he couldn't deny the excitement the offer generated as he watched the don walk toward him. He could see the change in the dedoochka, the anger behind the glazzies, which suddenly didn't seem as tired, the flaccid rot and shiyah, which somehow had firmed into a semblance of the man he remembered. Even the leaden gray litso took on the color of health.

"You pony what happened tonight, yes, Lord Perrineau." It wasn't a question the way Pavarotti said it, but a statement. "We got tolchokked real horrorshow. The full Menap take, I lose a few droogs in the heist and the sloppy bums that did it also kill a couple of the rozzers."

It was the first Perrineau had heard of this. He had received a video call and was told to get over to the old man's house at once but nothing more was said. Now as he sat staring up at Pavarotti's wrath, his rassoodock clicked like a computer, calculating the significance.

"The full take," the lord said aloud thinking of the amount of pretty-polly it must have been. But Perrineau knew it was snuff. Whenever the Syndicate was hit in the past, and this was rare, they all had the same endings written off in red ink, but their code, their very foundation, dictated that the ink would be supplied by the blood of whoever had done it. Now Lord Perrineau of Cambiocorsas as he now says of himself, in which he is identifying himself by the better types of auto-trons that he is now *associated* with, knew the true meaning of why he was here. But the offer of this so-called possible jump in the Family seemed all but jive talk coming from old man Pavarotti. The Family didn't need a specialist on a kill like this. Rumors based on fact would filter through the organization, for everybody would be checking out the smell of fresh deng. He had no doubt that the perpetrators would be found; a day, a week, it didn't matter. Then whoever had done it would be dead, as simple as that. It didn't warrant a bonus, a simple press of a button to a video call was all it would take. The Family anywhere in the region could handle the execution.

Pavarotti spread his rookers, his palms up, as if his problems were too large and he was asking for help from some personal deity. "So what do I do, huh? Do I video call one of the brothers back at the cantora who's running the shit for us up there, give him a slap on the rooker and tell him, spare me some cutter, then let him go on like before and wait for it to happen again?"

Lord Perrineau knew Pavarotti didn't want any answers to a solution; solutions had been thought out beforehand by The Family and if they hadn't he was not going to suggest any, because if they went wrong he knew he might have to pay for them.

"Yarbles, great bolshy yarblockos to all of them, I won't have this!" The old man shut off his rage like a faucet, containing it in his glazzies, which compounded with the inner fury of his strategy. He sat down on the sofa again and leaned forward, his goloss lowering. "I'll tell you what the deal is; I'll teach them something they won't forget!" His thin fingers moved out of the silk robe and pointed like a pooshka aimed at Lord Perrineau's chest.

"I'm giving you the contract, Lord Perrineau. I want whoever pulled this shit off to lay dead forever." The don said just as a small black pug dog named Marionette just came right along and plopped herself up on the plushy couch where Lord Perrineau is sitting. She then makes her way comfortably and trots along the couch to sit above Perrineau's nogas.

Lord Perrineau lowered his glazzies to the marble-top serving table and his rooker fillied absently with the tass. He then pets the animal and smiles the whole time. Pavarotti shrewdly read the meaning of the lord's thoughts. "I know what you think, lord. You feel anybody could do that kind of a job, that I'd be wasting your talents." The dedoochka leaned back and shook his gulliver slowly. "But you're wrong. What I got in the ole rassoodock is going to take a specialist with lots of guttiwutts. This is exactly why I sent for you Lord Perrineau. This is going to be handled like nothing you ever done before because I'm sending you up there with just a few droogs to carry out the assignment."

Lord Perrineau didn't look up, not wanting the old don to see the problems he foresaw in this.

"And remember Lord Perrineau, you are acting in my name. Make me look real horrorshow huh!" exclaimed the boss-of bosses.

Lord Perrineau just kept nodding his gulliver in a sign of affirmation, thinking of how could he be sent on such a nebulous mission. He realized that his appearance would beset the satisfaction of those at the top. Something had to be done to find out who did it. But the old don had no patience with Lord Perrineau and this put worry on the man's rassoodock. Of course he would have to explain various situations to the ole dedoochka, tell him not to expect wonders and that this would definitely have to take some time. He looked up at the intense, haggard litso, again drained of color.

"What happens, Mr. Pavarotti, if we can't turn up anything? I mean this is a lot of town to go through, especially when someone doesn't want to be found." Lord Perrineau's soft, raspy goloss began subtly to manipulate the old dedoochka back to the standard procedures of reality.

"This was a hit by the Mussulmaun." The younger man's brow furrowed, the glazzies narrowing still further in his high-cheek boned litso. "How do you know it wasn't the Kohanim, aren't they usually the ones starting the entire cal?" snarled Perrineau not knowing exactly where this was going. He just couldn't see blaming ordinary lewdies for the hit on The Family.

"I don't know, I just took it for granted thought that it was an Anglo-Veck's heist."

"Yeah, I find it hard to believe, too." The old dedoochka was growing tired and cranky, "but I got a video call from Audubon. One of the rozzers he got on the payroll up there told him it was the Negro-Vecks that done it, that's why he's got to produce fast or he's going to be in a lot more trouble than he is right now. I won't have any bullshit!" The don stated his firm point. But Perrineau grew suspicion after the don had mentioned the name of Audubon and how he has a rozz on payroll. Perrineau didn't recall the wealthy Audubon having any newspeak of a rozz on payroll, if he did, why didn't he mention this to him before? The old don was up to something and this time his lies weren't adding up. The cough came suddenly to the old dedoochka and the force of it sent the man bending over with pain. His rooker groped inside of his robe carman for a handkerchief and he pressed it across his rot. Perrineau raised himself to offer some help, but Pavarotti just waved him back down again. The old don was stubborn. It took him a full minute to get his plot controlled again. His glazzies watered and he wiped spittle from his goobers. He was embarrassed by the sudden bout with indigestion and stood up, wanting to get away from Perrineau's stare of sympathy, detesting the pity he thought he saw in the dark glazzies of his subordinate. He paced the floor slowly, pushing back sickness by the remembrance of who he was and what he represented. And then he was the don again, the Mafioso head of an invincible Family, who had built his rank and reputation on ultra-violence and quick retaliation. He stopped in the middle of the floor, whirling around Perrineau. "I have been hearing about this Negro-Veck wanting a bigger piece of the take. But here's the thing, no matter who you put up there in charge it's going to be the same thing because when you get an outsider to run the shit for you, you're takin' a chance. They start to see all that money and they get bolshy shot ideas. The only way to keep these Negro-Vecks in their place is through fear! You know what I mean. You can't let too many of them get the upper rooker over you, especially the L-Comm."

Lord Perrineau's dark heavy eyebrows arched pathetically. He wasn't sure of where his passion set with all of this and at what side was he truly standing on anyway. Furthermore, he grew irritated with Pavarotti's sudden racism. But even furthermore, the whereabouts and past connections of Perrineau to his blood family who are also just as corrupt have long been kept a secret from Don Pavarotti all because business is still business. They were on their own terms and he was independent. Perrineau has no intention of telling Pavarotti how his actual father can have something to do with the heist. Lord Perrineau Basquiat was just that: A Basquiat. His father Gerard Basquiat has a lot of control of commissions in the city's drug game. Not only this, but Perrineau isn't exactly on the best speaking terms with his father since citing their irreconcilable differences of the mere existence of the Nuwaubian Moors and their immense control over Districts 5 and 6. So this just makes things more complicated.

"It's someone that we know closely." said Perrineau.

"I thought about that, too," Pavarotti answered, "but who in the hell could it be?" The old don's glazzies burned with avengement.

"I want you to operate out in the open, Lord Perrineau. No back alley cal on this one, because I want you to flash the muscle so everybody can see it. Let them pony who is running the show around here, let them know nobody goes against us and lives. I want this lesson given to them tonight while this thing is still the hot uptown newspeak. Go after the mother, a wife, father, I don't care who, just so long as you cut them open and lay them dead in the middle of the street."

Lord Perrineau stared up at the old dedoochka. Only minutes before he had doubted Pavarotti's competence, but now he was marveling at the quick retribution he had planned. It would be a brutal reprisal, but some veck had to do it. It didn't bother Perrineau that he might have to kill the innocent; they had been killed before while he was a secret operative for his father and that was almost classic, too. Now he knew why he was here, but he wondered if Pavarotti knew how easy none of this was going to be. It was a difficult contract from the beginning. Pavarotti needed to pony that two of the rozzers were tolchokked. Since this happened, more of the millicents were expected to team up with their own code of retaliation.

He listened to the old don filling him in on the take from several B-Loop drug and policy rackets, the gambling and loan-sharking, the string of titty bars, nightclubs and whorehouses, not to mention all the kickbacks to politicians and the rozzers that kept them in business, and finally on Hector's commission and how much it cost to maintain his black help to run more upscale cantoras. He watched the gray gulliver punctuate the words with gestures and nods, half-hearing the sick, hoarse goloss and thinking that he was being given a smell of the brimming, rich, corrupt pot, but only the lid would close before he had any opportunity to dip down into it if he didn't execute the man's orders.

A clop at the door brought the don to silence. Without waiting for an answer, Elena quickly entered through a door while holding Pavarotti's grandson Junior. The young malchick was dressed in short pajamas.

"Junior wanted to say goodnight before he went to bed," Elena said, acting as though Perrineau weren't there. The wizened litso of the old don broke into a grin, he opened his arms and the boy came running to him, then he closed them around the little boy, and the dark, haggard eyes flashed with unexpected vitality. But there was sadness, too. And it was possible to see tears as the don stared above the malenky ruffled head buried in his chest.

"What a malchick," Pavarotti said, "Some little boy you are eh."

CHAPTER 4

nside this circular tower standing 260-meters stood the location of the millicent headquarters which was built adjacent to the Capitol. It was an enormous beast of a headquarters and represented the round features such as that of the discus hotel, although more shelled in its appearance, which sat directly above the sea. One particular high-ceilinged room was lit by pale lights where along the walls hung various white-papered credentials of the Millicent Academy. Laptops and video call screens sat atop of desks fastened to fiber optics cables in what appeared to be a building that housed a Private Investigations and Millicent Unit.

A desk sergeant, Horace Bivens, presided behind the high desk as several of the rozzers speak openly about OPERATION TARMAC in a corner toward the rear. In front of him were the bedraggled and enraged prestoopniks that just got booked. It was a night of dratsing it was. The cells in the basement were being filled up by lewdies. Detectives worked upstairs in the cramped squad room, questioning the undesirables and informants they had rounded up for leads that would lend substance to the mumbling words of a dying man's cry: "Negro-Vecks, L-Comm!" someone yelled in the room. "I am not Negro-Veck, you motherfucker, I am Afro-Comm!" Another deep goloss screeched.

To Bivens, the patrolmen and detectives all seemed a soft blur as they passed quickly, some acknowledging him, others inordinately quiet, all sensing in the charged atmosphere that the Millicents have just arrived from dratsing. Bivens tapped a code to a video call screen as several individuals walked up to a multi-media device, looking into it, which would ID them. Their names appeared in the neon lit letters upon the digital flat screen and a silver door was pushed open. Behind the silver door is a long stretched hallway that resembled an entranceway to a clinic, but in actuality it is a locker-room. At the end of the long tunneled hallway, various rozzers could be seen moving about and talking with fierce jabbering as they put on the orange colored platties marked – OPERATION TARMAC.

"The ministry of truth or minitrue, in futuristic speech, was startling different from any other object in sight. It was an enormous octagonal structure, almost like a billboard, and it was quite possible to read, yes." said George Orwell as he put on his jumper pants, "It read, war is peace, freedom is slavery and ignorance is strength. I saw it!"

"Yes, yes, I pony this, I have money invested within the ministry of truth." said a rozz, Sean Cheadle, "although I have thought of switching my account to the ministry of peace, but yet still undecided, I suppose."

"Anything but the Bones and Skulls, that's for sure!" said Jason Flare closing his locker.

"Anything but The Staja Room!" George knows he's

trying effortlessly to speak over the loud chattering that's going on and continues slamming the locker doors to get his point across. They are not even sure they know what they are talking about since all members of the rozz team are much younger and inexperienced as the members of the millicent team. The rozzers are much younger and impressionable. Their role in the force is simply to take all makeshift weapons off the streets and maintain through the city as peacekeepers. But their youthful govoreeting feels like they are anything but of the molodoy in all thinking and consciousness. They are too young for their own good. Not mature at all. Suddenly a few friends come over to fancy a chat.

"And now were back to where we were again, yea? Just like before and all forgotten, right, right, right!" shouts Sean Headle. All the men slap high-fives to each other in a very tribal way. Georgie Boy slams into Sean Headle in a droog like way and says: "don't talk to me ya flea bitten drunk, I know what you've been up to."

Hot-headed Sean raises a fist, "yarblockos and you fuck off you flint-faced fag!"

"You no horrorshow pan-handle sucking bastard"

"Your mommas a scaly castrating banshee bitch!" The two are head to head now. Jason jumps in, "alright you two….both your dad's are horse asses."

Jason pushes into Georgie and then into Sean and they erupt into full-fledged dratsing. A circle emerges and its game-time only after awhile everyone can viddy that they are play-fighting and the interest discontinues.

"Well Georgie Boy, what's the idea you got for us tonight?" asked Sean.

"No, not tonight, not this nochy." responded a haggard George.

"Come, come, come Georgie Boy, you're a big strong chelloveck like us all. We're not little children are we, Georgie Boy? Come now; tell us, what do thou hast in mind for this nochy?" The men all gather in closely to hear of it, with a threat, too. A confrontation happens and the men blow off steam on each other as someone is pushing in the group real hard. The boys are very physical in their play fighting. Several fists square out into the air and a real competitive fight almost starts, but Georgie Boy is restrained and forced to speak.

"Okay, okay, alright!" Georgie Boy shuffles as they release him. "It's out there a bit out of town. Isolated. There is this large domy, it's owned by some very rich ptitsa who lives with her cats. The place is shut down for a few days and she is completely on her own. The place is all full up with gold, money and like diamonds and shit like that."

The boys all exchange gurgling sounds of enjoyment at the thought of a crast going real horrorshow this evening. It was good to work for the Capitol because you got the privileges of coming and going throughout any district without any security problems. They themselves were the security, but just as they were all discussing about this crast a video call screen appeared in mid-air. It appeared at first just to startle the boys and grab their attention, but then the lazers fell back into the wall which was its original design. Brother Barama-X appeared in the constricted green lazer frame of a large telescreen suspended up from this large wall. A large deafening sound blasts from all around the tunnel creating a series of echoes.

"Oh no, not the alarm, not the alarm!" screams Sean. He grabs his gulliver as he suddenly feels a migraine headache.

"I am having a double-think!" shouts Georgie Boy.

"Stop, stop, stop the alarm, please!" Jason Flare screeches.

In the large telescreen, Brother Barama-X's long and round Negro-Veck litso faded out. Fading back in the screen was the lining of soldier's boots as the sounds of rhythmic trampling formed the background around the three large capital letters, B-B-X. The vicious alarm pounded relentlessly through the PA system and amplified past the underground gates with no sign of stopping.

"I have pressed the Hate Button so that you can never forget. Big Brother Barama is watching you. And remember, you must never become an Overdrawn again. You don't want to become an Unperson, do you? I think not!" The goloss pierces through the loud speakers, so loud, that uncontrollable exclamations of rage started breaking out from half the chelloveks in the room.

"Now get to work, all of you, before I have you all gone!" Barama-X growled again, his goloss echoing profusely throughout the halls, which sent a horrible chill through the plotts of those forced to listen.

Immediately everyone gathered themselves and headed toward an elevator which would lead them to Room 100 down below as the alarm suddenly stopped. Five to six members of the Operation Tarmac team piled into the entrance way as the elevator doors opened. Jason Flare pushed the elevator button marked Room 100 and the silver doors closed. Then suddenly a women's voice was heard over the PA system inside:

Voice:

"May I have your attention please?
A newsflash at this moment arrived from
the United Iranian Front. Their claim is that
provocative words by
Big Brother Barama-X
and a fresh military buildup in the
Persian Gulf seem to mark a new focus by the
Members of Manep on Iran that could signal another C-11
or even a deadly confrontation."

The women's goloss repeated the same words over and over again for about three times and was followed by a series of trumpet sounds floating throughout the PA system. Then suddenly the elevator doors opened and all the teamsters piled out as they headed for their individual duties. The desk sergeant, Sgt. Curtis Mayfield, from his high perch glanced at the opened elevator doors and witnessed the Operation Tarmac team coming out, but then turned back to the prestoopnik who was being booked on charges of aggravated assault. The pimp standing before the desk sergeant had his kinky *luscious glory* straightened into a slick pompadour and his mustache was evenly trimmed over his upper lip. His chartreuse sports jacket was blood-splattered and he seemed bewildered.

"Were there any weapons on him?" asked Sgt. Mayfield with a goloss that seemed to carry indifference.

"Just this knife," responded the rozz. The sergeant barely looked up from his writing. "Was there any resistance when the arrest was made?"

"Yes, a little," he said.

"Where was he apprehended?" Mayfield's pen seemed to start across the blotter before the answer was given as if he knew of something.

"The mesto is called Korova Spacebar. It's over in District 5, yea," the rozz answered tonelessly. "My partner stayed with the car and I went in alone to avoid suspicion. There were a few Anglo-Vecks and Asian-Vecks mixed in with the crowd of Negro-Vecks and I didn't viddy anything out of the ordinary"—he motioned with his rooker to the ruffled Negro-Veck beside him—"until this veck comes out with a knife as one of his sookas gets caught in a bit of dratsing with the others over some so-called crast that happened before."

The sergeant's litso began to frown, "alright I've heard enough, you can take him down to the cell." The sergeant was going to compliment the efforts of the young rozz but suddenly felt he shouldn't be so facetious.

"Sergeant!" The goloss was loud; it startled him. Sgt. Mayfield turned quickly to the grimly serious litso of the rozz standing in front of the desk. It was Roger Valentine.

"What is it, Roger?"

Roger said, "The prestoopnik that I was assigned to cover at the Menap General Hospital has kicked the bucket." Mayfield realized that the rozz was well aware of what was happening and knew that the death of the only witness could only add unwanted agitation to an already precarious case. The sergeant prepared himself for a long, dreadful night ahead. He looked away from the dark, somber face staring intently up at him and started to fake some writing across the blotter.

"Captain Clarke is in interrogation," he said, not looking

up. Then, as if in casual afterthought, "you'd better go and tell him."

The interrogation room was small, without windows; a ventilating duct was cut crudely into the ceiling. A bright lamp with a reflecting shield at the top poured a circle of intense white light on the Negro-Veck who sat directly beneath it in a straight-back wooden chair. The heat of sweat and fear poured from the young man in the chair, beading his litso and wetting his luscious glory as if he had been doused with a bucket of water.

"So you say you lived in the place for over a year, is that correct?" He recognized the captain's goloss coming through the obscuring haze of smoke from the cancer sticks.

"Yes sir, I have." The answer came slowly, respectfully from the downcast gulliver.

"And you still tell us you don't know who used your flat this week or any of the people who were there?" The goloss of the captain sort of rankled in a tone of disbelief.

"No sir, I don't know any of them," the man insisted, "I am telling you, I—I don't know who they are or why they were there. I don't pony anything."

"Leroy, you're a goddamn liar!" The goloss of the captain climbed as so did his impatience.

"Look at me, Leroy!" The prestoopnik continued to stare at the floor.

"Did you zvook what I just said, I said look at me!" The captain shouted. Slowly the Negro-Veck prestoopnik lifted his gaze, his shining litso moving up into the harsh light. Sweat on his forehead formed into rivulets and rolled down the sides to his cheeks. His glazzies squinted and his litso tightened as though he was going to cry. The captain's plott slackened and he took a drag from his cancer stick.

"I am willing to believe that you are innocent for now, on all counts except one. It was your apartment where the killings took place and you have to know at least one of the shaikas. I am sure this wasn't the first time your place was used as a pickup. Basquiat uses a lot of different spots that he feels are safe to do his business. He moves them around to keep people guessing, and your apartment is one of them. I even heard that he was one of the fewest Negro-Vecks to enter District 1. Hah, the nerve! It makes no sense for you to be busted on a big charge, because you're protecting something we already know about."

Clarke paused and waited and took a step back to ease the prestoopnik's apprehension, but only cowering timidity came from the thin Negro-Veck who continued to hold his litso up into the light. Then he closed his glazzies as though hoping that when he opened them again the hot, shut-in room with its bright light and questioning Anglo-Veck captain would somehow have disappeared.

The captain turned and stepped over to a shadowy figure leaning against the wall. Their words were chumbled whispers; then he came back to the cowering man, who again had let his gulliver drop down toward the floor. Slowly Clarke lit a cancer stick and held it out to the Negro-Veck, who took it in a noticeably nervous hand, then quickly filled his lungs with its momentary comfort.

"Mr. Lovelace, I'm prepared to offer you a deal, and under the circumstances it's more than you could hope for. Leroy, you give us what we want and we'll give you a clean record. We can have your chip re-loaded and have your crime history erased. You can upload a new clean life." The prestoopnik raised his gulliver, his glazzies seeking Clarke, who stood just outside the perimeter of light.

"We need a signed statement telling us how you were contacted, how much the brothers paid you the cutter and how many times Basquiat used your apartment as a drop for the drencrom." The captain continued. The expression on Leroy's litso still held the anxiety, but his glazzies narrowed against the trail of cancer smoke as he pondered the new proposal, which would free him from the stink and dread of this silver box of a room.

"I can pony why you let them use your mesto. Why would you let the Nuwabian Army control you Leroy? Don't you know what they are capable of? By golly just look at Proximus Centauri, can't you see you Negro-Vecks don't stand a chance? The cutter they gave you must have been enormous to your advantage I am sure. You weren't hurting anyone right? They come and go and you don't viddy them until another time, yea? If this didn't happen tonight, Mr. Lovelace, why I don't even think we would know you, or knew that you ever existed. You just happened to be unfortunate for the timing. Your place was marked for the knock over. This misfortune has placed you in a very baddiwad position. But you can pull yourself out of it; you can get out clean, just by giving us a simple statement of facts. All we want is a signed statement."

The prestoopnik's gulliver seemed too heavy for his thin body and he lowered it so that his chin was almost resting on his chest and he gaped at the floor as if he were deaf and incapable of comprehension.

"Don't you behave like the animal farm, I am giving you

an out. If you're not smart enough to realize it, it doesn't stop us from getting what we want. We could always say there was an accomplice rap in here somewhere. Just attach it to something else just as related. You know you all behave like the animal farm."

The rozz standing in the shadows cleared his gorlo before govoreeting and Clarke turned toward the gesturing.

"Welly, welly, well, I do beg your pardon, sorry for the oobivat," said the rozz, it was actually Roger Valentine— the rookie. He had been waiting for the proper moment to interrupt the interrogation and had become so immersed in watching the pressuring of the uncommunicative prestoopnik that he wondered now whether he'd waited too long.

"What?" Clarke asked impatiently.

"The prestoopnik, sir, the one marked real horrorshow to the crast—well he kicked the bucket before they could get him into surgery. You know the one, yes?" said Roger, "we didn't get any chance to get a statement before he went out."

Clarke stared at the young rozz for a spell as he eased out of the room. He had hoped for a quick resolution from a dying man's declaration that would give them leads to corner immediately. He turned back to the prisoner. Lovelace was just a grab-bag surprise, a bonus he had intended to use against the seemingly untouchable Basquiat. For years Gerard Basquiat had flaunted connections to The Party. He was legally immune with a business front while yet and still he was capable of instilling fear among those who would dare inform against him.

And now he finally had him through an insignificant prestoopnik sitting terrified as ever. Basquiat was the bolshy achievement, the one that the lewdies would remember him for. And all that would be needed to start it was a signed statement from Leroy Lovelace. The district attorney would issue a grand jury indictment that could expose all the vices and corruptions that sucked the ghettoes of Menap and good ole' Gerard Basquiat *King of the Nuwabians* would be brought before the Tribunal. It was the kind of raskazz that the gazettas would love and exploit, and from the investigative explosion, cankerous fallout would rain down on those responsible who hide on the periphery behind their full bag of take money. The chain reaction could knock over politicians and crackle right into headquarters, forcing the premature retirement of those behind all of the scandal. Yes, they'd remember him all right, and it would all be started by the testimony of a cringing Negro-Veck who admitted his dealings with the Nuwabian forces. Clarke could smell the indictment; could almost hear the cell door clanging on the convictions that would follow.

The obscure forms standing back in the darkness sensed the change in the captain, in the way he stepped under the light and pushed his litso down to the prestoopnik.

"Okay, Leroy, we're through playing games. I told you I'm prepared to let you out of this. You won't do a day. Your only involvement would be a simple statement on how you were being used." Clarke waited for an answer, but the bowed Negro-Veck remained stubborn and held his gulliver down. The back of Captain Clarke's hand struck across Leroy's litso. One of the rozzers standing in the back stepped into the light and pushed Leroy back into the chair. Once more, the fist of the captain pulverized Leroy's stomach and he fell over. The rozzers continued grabbing him and roughing him back into the seat. Clarke's rooker caught Leroy's litso across the rot, forcing his zoobies to cut into the goobers. They started to bleed.

"Sign the paper, now!" Clarke demanded with a growl of anger. He struck Leroy again and again, spinning his gulliver and sending a spray of blood out across the brightness. Blood leaked from his smashed rot and rolled down across the captain's fingers. "You're going to sign it!" Leroy heard the Anglo-Veck captain's demand.

"You can smash at me all you want, but I'm not signing nothing because I ain't going against Gerard. He's got too many lewdies behind him, yea. He'd have me killed real quick and I would rather do time than be dead." Leroy said.

Captain Warren Clarke continued to hold the prestoopnik's jaw, but was suddenly unsure of his depth, afraid of this swift, unexpected current of truth. He could still see trepidation etched across the battered litso, but the glazzies were laced with straightforwardness. There weren't many prestoopniks who were victorious in this small silver boxed room, but this frail and bleeding, insignificant man had succeeded. He rode it out on a fear of what a man named Gerard Basquiat could do to him that far surpassed the intimidations of a local department captain. Clarke took out a handkerchief and wiped the drops of blood from his rookers. He cleaned his fingers slowly, methodically, still staring down upon Leroy Lovelace.

"Book this faggot." The irritation came rolling out from Clarke in a tone of bitter frustration. The door surprisingly opened as someone had just entered the secret pass code; the occupants seemed frozen in their positions. It was Sgt. Mayfield.

The sergeant took a step further into the room. "Captain I have the night tour and they are ready to go out now."

They stood in regimental form as they had gone through roll call. They were at attention; their dark colored uniforms were already clammy against the night. Their pooshka belts hung around lithe plotts and the shlemmies were squared tight above their glazzies. Some turned their gullivers slightly, others their glazzies, as they followed Clarke. They watched him mount the couple of steps and move behind the railing. They didn't particularly take any notice to the other rozzers who had come out of the interrogation room and now stood authoritatively against a back wall. The captain, his glazzies showing strain behind the otchkies, scanned the litsos of the ruddy, the swarthy, the pale and the black, all glistening with sweat.

Some averted their glazzies while some stared back insolently, but most returned his look with a passive indifference that reached up across the desk and slammed gallingly against Clarke's indignation. He could feel the acrimonious sting rising in his chest. It was his duty to speak about the loss of two rozzers, to touch briefly on the atrocious crast, then to let them go, for they weren't the investigators who would have to shift through the shit of the Menap underworld. Their purpose was to prevent crime by the show of a uniform on the street and if someone broke a law, it was their duty to bag and book him and let the so-called higher-ups put the case together.

"Some of you may have already known this, but we lost two of our patrolmen who were killed in the line of duty." Clarke leaned forward, his palms going flat on the desk. A silhouette in the corner from a lit lamp shade had shown the outline of the captain's moving plott as he spoke. "The backbone of the law is the person in the uniform. But his commanding image has slowly deteriorated in this society. So for the sheer necessity of gaining respect it is required that he gain it by exercising his authority, which is exactly what each and everyone of you will do this nochy."

There was a complete silence in the area as the captain spoke. His goloss raised high above to the upper marble and silver floors where various detectives came out of their squad rooms to stand on the marble steps.

"I want you men going out on this late night tour to send a message to those filthy muppets of the T-1 and Hunts People sections of the city and that we are serious. I want it sent to the whores and the pimps, to the sookas and their brothers, the pushers and the junkies in all of their after-hours joints and bottle clubs. It is the summoning or dissolution of our government and it is in furtherance of the executive power by Big Brother Barama -X to carry out this extermination. There will be gallows built in rows, then those overdrawn lewdies will be hanged indiscriminately, and they will remain until they stink; they will hang there as long as the principles of hygiene permit. As soon as they have been untied, the next batch will be sprung up, and so on down the line. Other districts will follow suit, precisely in this fashion, until all of Manep has been completely cleansed of these worthless gangsters. They don't even wear their under platties any longer, they just sag their bare bottoms out in the nagoy like the animal farm and defecate in public in their ignorant protests of not having any place to go." The captain made his point with exaggerations.

The flexible ranks now seemed to stiffen. There were no scowls or lethargic glances now by these rozzers who stood in their regimental form.

"The vast majority of the *petite* bourgeoisie in the community, like anywhere else, are honest, law-abiding citizens who want and need protection. And now these people of the social ruling class are going to be watching every move of the millicents. Trust me, you don't want this any other way guys. We're going in!"

What Clarke was saying had every bit of truth in it. The reality was that there hadn't been a single murder in over 30 years on the rozzers task force and now two lay dead. Together the millicent and rozzers were successful in confiscating every single murder weapon from the lower districts who were primarily blamed for all the senseless murders. All districts became safe for a number of years despite District 7 remaining as the worst. Many of the citizens within District 7 were not so law-abiding. Many citizens of District 7 just made their own weapons and distributed them through their channels of pride men.

For long seconds no one moved in the oppressive silence, not realizing he had finished. Then Mayfield, conscious that his commands were too loud in that quiet hall, turned and moved the rozzers out onto the streets of the night. Clarke watched as the millicent ranks disappeared through the doors.

The Kingdom of Ettok, its telescreen and bright lights snaking around the electric neon sign was located in the A-1 parish of District 5. It was one of the few remaining parishes that still drew Anglo-Vecks from the higher districts. But their number had fallen off since the bombings and the riots and it was mostly well-heeled Negro-Vecks from the mid-level districts who got out of their expensive ETV mobile pods and auto-trons tonight in front of the canopied entrance. Tonight is the celebration of Big Brother Barama-X's daughter's wedding and she felt droogy enough to hang with the movers and the shakers on her special weekend celebration. Barama-X was the first Negro-Veck to be appointed as the Leader of the Capitol of Manep even though he is half-Irish and a descendant of the Drogheda Monarchy which was looked at suspiciously as a possible enemy to Manep. The doorman, his white admiral's uniform laced with elaborate decorations, salaamed humorously to the modish women and shuffle-danced the men toward the entrance. Once they left a mobile pob at the curb entrance, the doorman would snap his fingers to a waiting attendant and majestically would motion them to take it away to a lot around the corner. But sometimes that grew to be a problem too because it often became overcrowded, so the valet boys would double-park the vehicles along the streets. The doormen were a show-off for sure.

Inside the Palace of Ettok, heavy soul guitar rhythms and hard rock drums were playing. It was The J-Fetish band on stage warbling the psychedelic Doo Doo Wop song, on the *misa digital*. Candles flickered on a few tables along the wall, making litsos barely distinguishable in its reddish glow. A few lewdies were let in through the iron gated door in the basement. It was the type of mesto where you knew where you stood. If someone got sloppy with drink or was nasty or too old, they personally got thrown out by Gerard Basquiat's Nuwabian droogs. The notorious and ruthless

Basquiat ran his nightclub without district permission and could care less about nothing more than only business. This was an after-hours joint that had no closing hours and the drinks were the strongest ever. The customers knew what they came for before they even stepped foot onto the carpet. A tray with a platter of ham hocks, turnip greens and smoking black-eyed peas topped with rice was being pushed through a crowd of Negro-Veck socialites courting their *mediumship* meetings as other couples danced into the musical evening.

Two Negro-Vecks, Isaac Payne and Gary Overdrawn adorned in fashionable white and red-trimmed sport suits, stepped down into a red carpeted stairway with its lavish ornamental balusters that spiraled down a few floors. They headed down a long dimmed hallway where Isaac Payne, tapped a secret code with his knuckles against a blackened door. On the other end, Sheila Foxtail looked through a peephole, but gasped in shock because she didn't recognize the guys and this secret knock pattern. Sheila was a tall, slender and beautiful jet-black cheena of Jamaican and Native American ancestry in her twenties. If she wasn't out robbing, killing, stashing or flashing, she would be either gambling dice or selling her high priced pussy. She didn't just sell to anyone; Sheila was a high class cheena and rolled with the head honchos who had big money to throw.

The silencer of a pooshka clicked off as Gary shot his silence enabled gun which popped off the doorknobs. The front door was burst open allowing Isaac and Gary to barge in quickly.

"Now I don't want no trouble. I pay my ice the first and the fifteenf!" Sheila said with much consternation in her goloss as she fell backwards to the edge of a sofa. The commotion from the door slamming into Sheila's face and the dramatic entrances of the two gun wielding men sent Sheila into a spell of wild formations. Blood began to stream down her nose.

"And I'm all square and I got my paid-up connections, so don't you two be disruptin' my business."

Two Anglo-Vecks, Georgie Boy and Jason Flare sat apprehensively on the edge of the sofa looking at Isaac and Gary with weary glazzies. Jason motioned to Georgie Boy to get going and they both headed for the door.

"Now where you malchicks going? You sit right down, you hear, it won't be long. I'll have a couple of my gals ready for you in just a minute. It'll be worth your wait; these sookas are just what you both need, a good time!" Sheila insisted. She then turned to Isaac and Gary as the two Anglo-Vecks made themselves comfortable back on the sofa again.

"What'd ya want?" Sheila panted.

"What do you mean you don't know where Grenique is and where's the cutter?" Isaac said threateningly.

"Yarblockos!" Gary shouted.

"What cutter?" Sheila answered. Her glazzies squinted suspiciously and she started to shake her gulliver in denial. Suddenly she remembered that this was the droog from the crast. He had found her. She just remembered that there was another one of the same droogs who was there at the scene of the crast back at the domy some time ago but she couldn't remember if he had gotten shot by Yogita or even if he was dead for that matter. This whole thing was Grenique's idea anyway. She was always coming up with cal and then leaving it up to the other girls to clean up the left-behinds like this. She couldn't pony for a second as to how these droogs knew it was them who committed the robbery in the first place. Wasn't the make-up heavy enough to hide their identity? It was supposed to be like masks, another Grenique idea. Sheila remembers the very argument she had with her over how they were going to disguise themselves for the hit. Well this didn't matter; Sheila didn't have any money for like what these vecks were talking. The only money that she had was the payment from the in-out_in-out that she was paid earlier and it was "hold cutter" for Basquiat.

Suddenly everyone heard footsteps along a back hallway and grew silent. A silky curtain that hid the rear bedrooms was slid back and out came a ptitsa wearing a cheap rayon robe tied tightly about her waist. She had just run a comb through her tight bushy luscious glory and her feet scraped the ground as she dragged in her toofles. She appeared average looking and was nothing like her roommate who drew all the rage with her high-cheek boned beauty. The young ptitsa, named Honey Pen, (short for Penelope) looked no more than nineteen; her features were plain and her skin more white than brown. Most likely she was a mulatto child. Her bored glazzies made her look a lot older as she looked over the men in the room, apparently thinking that they were a couple of new johns.

"You just go back in there and cool off, Honey," said Sheila, "I'll call for you in a minute."

"Sheila your nose is bleeding." Honey Pen spoke softly with concern. Her goloss slurred like that of a person addicted to a drug or heavily under the influence of something strong.

"Go-on now, I get to ya in a minute." Sheila insisted as she wiped her litso with a nearby cloth.

As the young girl disappeared behind the silky curtain, Gary Overdrawn took his chance. He moved in close to Sheila and pulled her by the gorlo slamming her against a wall. Simultaneously, the two Anglo-Vecks Georgie Boy and Jason Flare bolted up to their feet from the sofa once again and left out the main entrance of the room running in a panic in regards to what was anticipated to happen.

"Don't fuck with me bitch, I'll slice you up like a steak, now where is the cutter!" said Gary.

"I don't know." Sheila replied. Gary rose up a balled fist and repeatedly began to pulverize Sheila's litso while Isaac continued to vandalize the room with spray paint. There was evidence of drencrom everywhere; burnt out needles, pipes, lighters, cancer sticks and the like.

"Oh you know where, bitch! It's crunk with drencrom in here and you don't know nothing, what's in that rassoodock of yours!" Isaac teased Sheila who held in her boohoo and wiped vino from her bottom lip. She is used to this type of treatment and vows her revenge one day.

"I got my men out bird-doggin' the area bitch; you better watch your ass!" Gary backhands Sheila and throws her down onto the sofa for the old in-out_in-out. He removes her under platties and rubs his rookers up and down his pan-handle near below his space pants. As they lay on the sofa half-naked, Isaac watches Sheila dratsing about with Gary while he is slamming on top of her.

"Remember that heist you pulled on top of that fucked up killing a couple of days ago, woman, The Party is starting to worry about you. You got everybody thinkin' that ya losin' ya juice baby, lettin' things run too lose now," whispered the conniving Gary to Sheila as he continued having forced sexual intercourse upon her. Sheila makes gurgling sounds as if she is choking, but really it is Gary with his fingers around her gorlo that is causing her to make these gulping noises. Isaac adds his two-cents, "yea, thought we didn't notice you under all the makeup and wigs huh?"

Up and beyond a haze of smoke was shown a revolving light inside the upper floors of the palace. Up past the pyramiding bottles in the center of the circular bar through more haze and smoke, was even more light and loud talk. Dobby looking devotchkas on cushioned stools, their gleaming gullivers moving with the tempo, and men in cosmopolitan suits, standing beside them or dancing, reaching for laughs with movements of exaggerated humor around quick bartenders and hustling waiters, diluted booze and crowded tables.

Then it happened. Zvooks of sharp creeches were suddenly heard from down below where a crowd had formed. A doo wop and rock group, The Jay-Fetish, had just taken the stage and the crowd of people began singing the lyrics of Now It's Gone out loud:

"If I could help you I would to figure out,
What you wanted
Inside my mind, never understood
Your values wanted
You said you'd be mine
Any and every and all the time
Shadows falling so sublime

Sing to someone else's song
Until the end, now its gone
Is there a party over here
Or is the party over there."

The room went dark, then a bright spot flared through the smoke, and lights came up from beneath the marbled stage as the group Jay-Fetish performed to an enthusiastic crowd. The singer J-Fetish—in which the band is named after their singer—was wearing purple glazzy shadow and black glazzy liner. He was a tall Negro-Veck man and looked healthy as any athlete. The all-male rock group sported dark herringbone jackets with V-cut collars turned outward. J-Fetish's magnetic sway pulled the dusky room to mesmerized silence as he played the guitar while warbling. Women's litsos hung transfixed above their drinks, each isolated in a common thought as their glazzies roamed greedily over the band adorned in their clever platties.

There was some sort of inside joke, which also was based in reality although The Palace was overpriced just enough as was the Korova Nightclub--it was to appeal to some of the newly arrived Negro middle class. However, its patrons were mainly a crowd of well-heeled dope dealers and numbers people, bookies and cheenas who'd broken through and had some illicit bag of connections going for themselves, as well as the wanna-be and hangers-on who still hoped to make it illegitimately.

CHAPTER 5

I t was the tight red pumps that detective Philip Stoner first saw here at this particular bar in the B-Loop. Candy was on the thin side, but the flashy dress swelled and curved in the proper places. She had turned her gulliver, listening intently to some guy, but following his quick motion, picked detective Patrick Magee out across the way.

"We shouldn't have to wait too much longer for this," said Stoner, "here she comes now."

"Will you shut up!" exclaimed detective Magee, "and don't blow our cover."

Magee turned and watched her approach. There was an outward appearance of calm, but as she came closer he could see concern in her gesturing. Her jaw line had a delicate firmness that accentuated the full, almost sensuous lips. Her luscious glory wasn't too long and was pulled back from her litso. In all, she appeared to look Oriental.

"Welly, welly, well, someone I hear is looking for something," she came off arrogant to Magee. Her goloss was unruffled.

"We are looking for Candy Lee." Said Stoner.

"That would be me." Candy said walking over closer and flashing her dragon themed tattoos as she removed an overcoat and spread it across the back of another chair to sit down. A few people had turned from their conversations along the bar and were staring curiously at the three of them. Magee reached out and pulled an empty stool between Stoner and himself and motioned for the ptitsa to sit down. She seemed thankful for the partial obscurity, which made her feel less conspicuous. The detectives watched her open her bag and dig down for some smokes. Neither man offered her a light; they watched her fumble for matches and light up. She looked at them; all traces of any smile had left by now.

"You'll have to excuse me; it's not every night I jeopardize my job by govoreeting to the millicents." Candy remarked.

"What makes you think that we are millicents?" Stoner asked.

"Rozzers, millicents, what the fuck ever, same cal!" Candy gabbed back. "So what'ya want!"

"We want to talk with you about your boyfriend, Audubon." Magee said.

"Ex-boyfriend!" Candy slammed. She studied the inflexible litso; his guarded glazzies offered no key to his feelings. Dropping her gaze, she took a long drag on the cancer stick and began walking. Magee and Stoner followed without being asked to.

The three of them were inside Candy's domy which was just a short gooly from the bar. Nervously, Candy pulled up a tass of brandy to her goobers as she sat across from them near a table. Some spilled over as she was shaking; her rooker nearly dropped the whole tass onto the floor. Candy Lee initially was a law student and had attended Menap Law School studying to become a real estate attorney at the height of the land boom. A very smart devotchka, she found it satisfying and hoped one day it'd be financially rewarding. But to her excuse came the collapse of the market. Developers went bankrupt, banks went under and that wasn't good for any real estate law student to aspire to in her rassoodock. So Candy used this low-ended excuse and dropped out to become a sooka. Mostly she just used this excuse along with her other stories to cover up her own laziness to study and finish school. It was during this time that the full-time call girl had met and had an affair with Audubon Kissel, who was and still is a married moodge.

"Now, I'll ask you again only this time I need a straight answer from you." Magee didn't raise his goloss.

"Now wait a minute, fellas, please." She pleaded. Her rookers held out loosely in a stop signal. "Can we slow it down a bit, huh? You're going a little too fast for me because, if I remember correctly, that dude is doing time and if he got out of the barry he sure enough didn't come running to me I can guarantee this." Magee and Stoner looked at each other briefly, and then back at her.

"We didn't say anything about him serving time." Magee stated.

"Mister, you don't work in a profession like this without knowing what's going on. Every pusher man, big and small, makes the scene around B-Loop one time or another and they all carry heavy okay, please…..I know what I am govoreeting. They don't call me the Young Lady of Asia's Four Little Dragons for nothing."

From their stares Candy knew they weren't satisfied with her vague answers. She would have liked to leave it at that and have them get out immediately for it was no one's business but her own. But they were The Men, and she knew she had better answer their questions or risk retaliation.

The cancer stick moved closer to Candy's red painted goobers as she took a long drag. It seemed that she needed to take a moment to gather her rassoodock.

"I can remember the first time that Audubon had gotten arrested for *carrying*. It was just around the same time that he was supposed to be promoted from a Fellow Craft to a Master Mason. He was of course let out by the boys and they somehow erased his records or something like this. I don't know exactly how it was, but it was something related to him being connected to the labor activists along with Gerard Basquiat and other party members—."

"You mean his involvement in the latest scandal of privatized intimidation along with Luciano Pavarotti," Magee interrupted.

"And who are the boys that you are referring to, miss?" said Stoner.

"Whatever…I don't really know all that cal!" Candy sighed. She got up without saying a word to fetch something and came back with what appeared to be two portable tube holders. She uncorked the lids and pulled out several large blue sheets.

"These are the blueprints that show the secret missions

brought under the command of the Drogheda Provisional Order. As you can see they are building human extermination chambers underground, underwater. It's a sick, sick world!"

"I heard about this," said Magee taking a closer look as Candy laid the blueprints across a black center table.

"Look there's Hunts People." Stoner pointed out with his index finger.

"And there's T-1 here." Magee added as he adjusted his glazzies under the sharp light."

"As you both can see, through all that cyanotype they are planning on building human extermination chambers right underneath the housing projects, or at least adjacent to it. They plan to exterminate the poor and the prestoopniks of Menap guys. Soon all major districts throughout Manep will follow suit if they haven't already thanks to that fucking marionette leader everyone elected, Barama-X." Candy growled.

"I don't get it, why don't they just arrest them and put them back in the barry?" retorted Stoner.

"The barries have been over capacitated for more than twenty summers now, haven't you to know!" Candy said. "The millicents have had it with District 7."

"And how did these blueprints get into your possession?" Magee asked.

"Audubon left them by mistake at my other place." Candy admitted.

"When?" asked Magee.

"I don't know. It was many moons ago."

"Before he got arrested?"

"Is he planning on getting these back?" Stoner interrupted.

"Maybe."

"He was never arrested was he; the whole thing is a cover up isn't it?" Magee sounded impatient, he wanted answers. The exhaled smoke rose above her gulliver. "Look, okay, I am scared out of my ass for telling you even this much. I won't deny that Audubon is a quack like all the rest of those party members, anyone of these ptitsas around here will tell ya that. But that was then and this is now and we stopped seeing each other. It was no fight or anything like that; he just stopped comin' around the club and that was the end of it. Just passin' time; a few laughs, you know, nothin' serious. It was a little while after that I hear he got messed up with the law and got sent away." Candy tilted her gulliver toward Stoner and shrugged sadly. "And that was the end of Audubon as far as my life would ever be concerned with, until you mentioned his name earlier, the man was completely out of my rassoodock."

"Well we sloosh he's back on the street and was seen about a month ago with his zheena, and this was told to us by the same dude who said you were his young mistress." Magee spoke slowly, watching her glazzies for a response, but there was only firmness that helped attest to her denial of everything.

"Well I can't help what you sloosh; I am fuckin' thirty-three falls now, a grown devotchka. I know what I am talkin' about here. If somebody says they viddy him with me within the last month or so, or any time since we stopped datin', they're puttin' you on. Why they mention my name with his now I sure enough don't know. But it's playin' a stupid trick on me, and I don't appreciate this at all."

The two detectives took a moment to access all of

the information. Magee looked at Stoner with an odd expression. Magee felt for some reason that Candy was hiding something. He just couldn't accept the fact that this ptitsa was telling everything that she knew.

"You won't have the millicents take me in?" Candy asked her goloss almost child-like.

"No-no, it hasn't come to this, but we do have more questions. You never said exactly what Audubon was carrying that got him arrested." Magee said.

"DRENCROM!" Candy yelled finally, "and loads of pretty polly too." She got up and began pacing the floor.

"He was doing business with the Kohanim. It was top secret. The AIC was also involved—."

"Wait what's this AIC?" Magee asked. Candy's glazzies flickered strangely in Magee's direction although she was looking at them both, but in deep thought as well.

"It's the CIA spelled backwards, but don't say it out loud, they maybe listening."

"Whose they?" Magee asked.

"Them!" she replied.

"Them who?" Magee asked again, "be more specific!" he insisted.

Candy ignored any further requests by the detective fumbling around the table for some odd distraction.

"It's possible that I am being watched by them as well for my involvement with Audubon and all this cal that I have on him." Her red heel pivoted and she turned to feed a large fish tank.

"Audubon is behind helping mastermind the killings of several labor activists. It's all over the cutter me brothers, truly it is." She reiterated to their fastened curiosities.

"I'd say he's one busy man then." Stoner joked while glancing around looking at photos and strange artwork throughout the apartment.

"Oh that's not it at all, the dude is dishonest, a complete loon, and I don't know how I ever got mixed up with him."

"So let me see if I pony all that you say. Audubon was some kind of treasurer with The National Association of Housing Cooperatives where instead of rearranging the financing plan to create a reserve fund and pay for renovations, he siphoned more than 20 million dollars into his own account, by forging signatures of those closest to him?" Magee asked, scratching his gulliver too.

"He arranged mass killings detective!" Candy said.

"Of whom? It seems a stupid story all drawn up. First a person rearranges an area for poor people to live affordably. Then after luring these same people into the same area he sells them drugs but actually he then takes their money, don't give them the drugs they just bought but then exterminate them in a series of mass killings?" Magee was sarcastic.

"The labor activists and drencrom dealers, haven't you been listening to what I have been saying all this time?" Candy argued.

"What you have been saying all this time Ms. Lee, is a cheest a' cal! Including the part where you claim that the only way for Manep to have the first Negro-Veck president is if we re-write the history books, come on!" Stoner blabbed interrupting.

"Now you know why he is working against the Drogheda Provisional Order, to make sure there never is a Negro-Veck president after this one." Candy stated.

"Who?" Magee asked.

"Audubon Kissel, who else, it has only been since the Ripening of the Moon that Barama-X was placed chief in command ya know. In a short time, history books can be erased, thrown out, burned out of the libraries and they can...."

"They can what?" said Magee, "and what's this Drog Provison's Order, or whatever you call this?"

Candy Lee pays no attention to the requests, her video call screen was buzzing and she had better answer it, it could be her pimp wanting to know her whereabouts. As Candy approaches closer to the medium sized video flat screen her tick-tocker races fast. She presses a little green square marked *okay* on the flat screen to accept the call, but then her tick-tocker resumes back to normal again as she sees that it is only some sort of advertisement for a local rock group. In an instant, a flicker of blue light fills the corner of the room and music is combined with a voice-over and backing track that sounds something like with horns and string instruments. A black character, his hair shaped in a Mohawk, comes into view on the screen top and speaks. Near the side of him is an animated version of the Octagonic Angel expressing her eight magical ideas for the moment:

Voice:
"Goo-ood evening cyber girls and
boys through the electrodes.
It is yours truly, J-Fetish, and I am
happy to announce Afropunk
night at The Korova Spacebar
Nightclub in just a few days.

A festival brought to you by the Droid
Control Marshals where there
will be two-for-one Penthesilea drinks
all night and a DJ after-party.
Come ready to get your groove on as I
will be playing with my band.
Cybermail your reservations quickly to
be one of the first ten selected
for a chance to party with me at the
Leopard Plaza VIP room.
You know the rules, no Isis Blades or Neteru Daggers...."

Candy expresses immediate enthusiasm all of a sudden
as she responds to the news, "Oh my gawd I love the J-Fetish
band!" She jumps up and down like a child and continues to
ignore the detectives hoping that they will leave.

It was early morning and the sun was shining bright
through the half-closed curtains within a room. Small
sparkles of yellow light danced along the walls decorated with
French African paintings, Native American sculptures and
large nzinga mirrors framed in brown that matched fluffy
pillows and gold trimmed tables were also a delight. The
okno, slightly opened, invited a refreshing breeze inside the
room and allowed unwanted scents to escape also. Anyone
could tell that the owner of this domy definitely suffered
from having a *Pharaoh complex* with all of the Egyptian
artifacts along the table fixtures, walls and carpeting.
    A ruby silk-colored kimono had been placed at the edge
of a rather large canopy bed sometime earlier and next to it
laid Grenique fast asleep in her matching ruby velour panties

and top. The comforter was thrown to the side a bit and her nogas stuck out. Suddenly some sort of strange shoom was made coming from the living room and Grenique woke up to the crashing sounds. Her tick-tocker began to race hard, *what the fuck was that*, Grenique messeled to herself. Without hesitation she pulled out of bed grabbing her kimono and went to her nightstand to retrieve a weapon but retrieved a dildo instead, *fuck*. With skorry she traded the long thick black instrument for a pooshka and spun it to the ready. Holding it forward, Grenique crept out of the bedroom towards the living room where she thought she may have heard the sounds that disrupted her spatchka.

Onto a Persian rug which covered the hard-wooden floor in a hallway, she edged her way to the living room and saw that no one was there. As she turned to make her way into the nearby kitchen she spotted the culprit. None other than Lord Perrineau himself was cleaning up fruit and broken glass that fell to the floor.

"God-damn you Perri, you scared the cal out of me!" Grenique bellowed. Lord Perrineau cringed at the sight of a gun being pointed at him. "Put the blaster down girl, it is only I!" the lord creeched back as he clumsily knocked fruit over. A few thumps could be heard as melons and apples splat the linoleum floor.

"The hell it is you!" Grenique said as she lowered the pooshka wiping sweat off her forehead. "How come you haven't answered my calls, Mister?" Her litso frowns at the site of the alabastrite stone-finished base to her favorite glass fruit bowl now broken in pieces.

"When?" he asked checking his portable video call screen, "I don't see any missed calls from you," he lied.

Before he knew it, Grenique was fast coming with a rooker slap toward his litso, but he grabbed her rooker just in time.

"Girl you better watch it!" Lord Perrineau said.

"What? You are in my domy motherfucker and I should kick your ass for scaring me like that." She huffed.

Lord Perrineau took a long hard look at his cheena, her beautiful dark brown litso frowning and sweating from the scare. He knew better than to piss this chick off. She is a tough person and doesn't back down from any dratsing. But yet he had a lot of worry himself. Just coming from the odd meeting with Pavarotti not too long ago and succumbing to demands by the big boss—the contract, the assignment, the Mussulmaun, the Kohanim—these pressures all played in the lord's rassoodock over and over again. He couldn't relax, had no one else to turn to but his baby girl, the sexy cheena. Before he stepped into the doorway of the domy he said a prayer to ward off any bad demons that may have followed. He had a key; it wasn't a problem even though they had their own separate places. Just a few hours ago he had walked into her bedroom and viddied her sleeping and didn't want to disturb her, but then got a little hungry and broke shit in the kitchen, was this a crime? How could she judge him now? It's not the first time he had come without calling. Why was she so upset?

"Baby, I am sorry. I know I should have called." Perrineau admitted while stroking her fine dark-brown colored luscious glory. She had dark red high-lights this time, but barely noticeable since her hair almost looked orange in some places too. He bent, took her rot hard and held her jaw with his rookers, then broke his hand away to begin kissing her litso frantically in hot, passionate bursts.

In one lithe move she began to remove his shirt, a sign that she wanted to make love. He didn't move or immediately say anything; all he could do was just allow his glazzies to drink her in. Gentle sunlight caressed the sheer kimono that she wore upon her shoulders. The illusion of her nude form, just the outline of her body sent Perrineau flying high into a world of lust and deep desire which caused him to grow a pan-handle. It was paralyzing to viddy where her groodies pointed so sharply, her nipples perking through the silk kimono and her hips positioned nice and tight upon tall nogas and healthy thighs. But still, she was shorter than the taller lord who stood well above six-feet.

"I need to strip by the door.....uh, it has been a long day yesterday and I haven't had a shower," he said quietly, ashamed to be so dirty in her presence. He looked at her and started peeling away the offending fabric.

"C'mon...let me get you a wash, baby," Grenique seduced. The lord didn't need to be spoken to twice. He allowed her to lead the way.

Low jets whipped the warm water within a tub and foam began to form where humidity in the bathroom had fog-coated the nzinga mirror and shower glass.

"Get in, all the way down to the shoulders....and lemme rinse the luscious glory," Grenique insisted.

If there was any dissention clinging to his spirit, it was pretty much taken away by the sudden heat Grenique had passed to motivate his will to follow her commands. He was agreeable to everything she wanted to do right now. There was no resistance in him whatsoever as he slid into the fragrant, opaque water and then immediately realized, while exhaling a sigh of pleasure, all of the silk mitts and loofah pieces which decorated the oval-shaped tub.

"How'z that baby," she asked him, her goobers sliding up and down his ooko and shiyah. She kissed his temple and continued to rub his back.

"Girl whatever it is that you are doing to me, please don't stop. I am in heaven right now, for sure baby." He replied as she nuzzled his cheek. It was the way that she did it while working the knots out of his shiyah with her thumbs underwater, then she'd rub her litso against his damp shiyah when he leaned up for her. He was trying as hard as he could to place his rot on hers, but she stayed behind him, just out of reach, alternately hard-nuzzling the sides of his shiyah until he arched in the tub.

No longer able to stand the tease, he turned real skorry to capture the nape of her shiyah with the cup of his wet rooker. He needed her yahzick to twine with his so bad now that when she opened her goobers to accept his kiss he moaned right into her rot. The sweet von of African musk incense filled the bathroom and he pulled her closer to him in which water splat to the floor. He stood up carefully not to trip over the fixtures as he looked at her now wet kimono clinging upon her beautiful curves. She stood with him for a moment, although he disrupted her plans, but it was okay for anything spontaneous was always welcome. The look on his litso was making her forget all that she intended to do with him. He couldn't help himself it seemed as he exposed his cinder block-defined chest, his beautiful abs and that dark silky trail of jet black voloss which curled just below his navel. The oils within the water had left his dark skin shining. The sunlight beamed through the oknos inside sending in a fireball charge between the both of them. It was magical.

As he led the way, she decided to run her thumbs over his dark, raisin-colored nipples and watched his glazzies slide shut. He swallowed hard as her rot found a scar.

"Eiiew, what happened to you here," she squealed at the site of a bruise that seemed like it just got there.

"Oh my God, what happened Perri." Her litso suddenly went into shock again. She was always so dramatic about things.

"Nothing woman….now come on let's go to bed."

Grenique's litso showed concern at this point with his sudden mood change. She didn't remember any scar the last time that she seen him, but she also couldn't remember the last day they actually made the whole in-out-in-out either. Grenique stared deep into his glazzies.

"You still working for them?"

"Working…for who—what are you govoreeting about now cheena!" He turned away.

"Luciano, Perri….are you still working for them?"

"Nawh, see Grenique there you go again with this cal!"

Grenique knew that in the Party System religion was the main cover-up over the entire scheme and the Bizango society is *Vodoun* which alone is an outcast. The Bizango also had a reputation to uphold. But at the same time Grenique could be extremely racist. Luciano was an Anglo-Veck and she didn't like Lord Perrineau operating with him and his White droogs. He was breaking the laws of the *Nuwabian Way* and she grew unsettled by this. Lord Perrineau thinks that Grenique is using the bruise incident as a way to get deeper into his business. She thinks that he is accusing her of him saying that the Nuwabian Way is growing more into fascism. She knew how bad his relationship was with his father, but then to make these accusations was overboard.

The young lord was definitely hiding something. His actions could only give this away. He was never truly a good liar and Grenique could always see that smirk in his litso when he was holding information down. All of his pressures were beginning to haunt him again. It was maddening. A rush of guilt produced goose-bumps up and down his body. He needed a distraction, any kind of excuse for that matter.

"Whooffsh...shit....I am cold," he complained. He grabbed a towel, "let's listen to some doobidoob." The lord went to a nearby radio and flicked it on. Then suddenly as the music filled the room vibrations of pleasure had sent Grenique far away from herself, out of body, out of her head, and out of breath to where ecstasy could exist in a sliver of universal fabric between one solar system and the next. She moved as the doobidoob echoed throughout the bedroom and she somehow met Lord Perrineau at the edge of the bed.

"I love you baby," the lord murmured. He pulled her closer to the bed and he blanketed her for it was an acute need that demanded this motion. He removed all of her clothes. His sudden weight upon her plot made her shimmer as her hips lifted to claim him. She was finally on her back. But just as skorry as he'd covered her with his hard plot, his shaft pulsing against her thigh like a promise, he withdrew back in order to position his goobers between her nogas. Her goloss bounced off the walls, her flat palm slapped the sheets, his back, and his shoulder, turning her nogas into a vise as pleasure hysteria lifted her up and wrung her out.

"Yes baby, oh my fuckin'...ooh aaahhh...." Lost for

words the cheena couldn't remember what her guy's name was for a moment. Ecstasy cluttered Grenique's rassoodock as Lord Perrineau's tongue wetted her some more. Her gulliver jolted back and her glazzies rolled back just as good from the thrusts. His tongue felt like nothing in this world. Now she remembers why she loved him so. If he wasn't a good man so-to-speak, he was definitely a good fuck this was for sure. Grenique had grins that reached ear to ear and her toes curled into foot-fists.

Then Perrineau, in one skorry move, rose up and grabbed her behind both knees. Grenique had to take one more peek at his long black pan-handle where she gasped at the strength of this monster. By the look of his glazzies Grenique could see that he really wanted to put it on her. Just as she had sensed this, she tensed up and immediately went into defensive mode; make-up sex after an argument could be brutal. Holding her rookers above her vagina she readied herself to push against Perrineau's stomach in an effort to control his depth.

As he entered, Grenique's back arched and her nostrils flared up. Her nogas were trembling uncontrollably which left her embarrassed. But little did she know the anticipation excited the lord even more. He loved how her toned stomach constantly contracted, the creases of her abdominal muscles rippling too.

Lord Perrineau matched Grenique's grip and he suddenly pummeled her real horrorshow. The bed sounded like it was going to snap at any given time as his noga knocked over fixtures on a nearby nightstand which sent everything crashing to the floor. He had to make his mark with her, seal the deal and make it plain. He felt that if he didn't, some other veck would try and that would be over his dead body. Good sex healed all wounds but the lord also had to make sure that Grenique knew that she was for him.

"Oh-oh shee-ee-it. Oh-oh my-ya-yi gaa-aah. I-I'm gonna-ah cuh-umm!" Grenique screeched. Her nogas shook like an old San Francisco earthquake from the old world and she struggled to open her glazzies. The sound of sweaty plotts and the moisture of a cheena's *down-under* being pelted by a pan-handle intertwined itself for a moment and was even louder than the doobidoob playing aloud. The bright sun had shown in through the sheers that hung at the okno. A small breeze came in right at the perfect time from the slight open of the okno and the bedroom door squeaked from the rush of wind that came with it. But the noise couldn't have distracted the couple's intense concentration to one another.

Not quite satisfied, Perrineau turned her over and positioned her to doggy-style. Grenique's luscious glory was shook out of place by now to the point where she looked like she might have been electrocuted. Appearing tired and worn-out, she took a series of deep breaths and prepared herself for round two. A rush of force knocked the wind out of her as the lord dug deeply into her derriere.

"Oh cal, holy cal b-bitch y-y-ou gonna m-make me cum-hum Nique!" The lord stuttered as he gripped his rookers onto her luscious glory, her gulliver pulling back. In an instant Perrineau pulled out his pan-handle and erupted a sea of semen onto Grenique's rear end; enough to lotion her plott completely.

"Shewwff," the lord said as his nogas trembled. No longer able to hold themselves up the two of them collapsed on the bed. Grenique was thankful the bed didn't break.

CHAPTER 6

The sky had darkened as it was well over eight o' clock. Yogita was waiting patiently at a table inside a restaurant and didn't want to appear too obvious that she was waiting for someone in particular. After all she was at the scene of a crast a few days ago and she never knew who was watching her. She fumbled around in her seat and stared outside the large oknos. Always conscious of her whereabouts, she could never settle her nerves. This is why she let Grenique run the show; call the shots. Yogita was dressed in micro-braids and usually you could find a bright-dimpled smile across her light colored litso.

A half-caste orphan of African and Iranian blood Yogita was younger and shorter than her sorority Neteru sisters which they called themselves. The Neteru was what the ancient Egyptians named their gods and these cheenas took on the identities of Egyptian goddesses, even though they were all born and raised in Menap. In their minds they were spiritual councils and delved into the beliefs of Ma'at, Netra and Heka. Ma'at is both the name of the goddess that bestowed order on the world after its creation, and the name of the metaphysical ideals governing everything from the rising of the sun, the position of the stars and the fate of all who walk the earth. Netra is the divine magic in which the gods possess as they go through *astral travel*, in other words traveling the paths of the ancient worlds. The pure fact of dreaming allows the god to visit unknown worlds and possess newfound strength. Heka is an ancient spell that is chanted:

Nuk Tem-Khepera keeper t'esef her uart mut-f.

The meaning is translated: *I am the uncreated god*. Each of these particular sorority sisters within their Neteru Council held little mini books in their purses which reminded them of these things and they swore by its truth, much more, they were goddesses no matter who didn't believe. But truly they were a foolish group of cheenas and easily brainwashed all at the same time. A secret loyal side operative to the Nuwabian Party was what they truly were, although they were in denial about this. In the glazzies of Grenique, Sheila and Yogita they were all independent. An even deadlier ensemble when it came down to the cutter. Although the Neteru members were many in quantities, it was just these three who stuck together as thick as a brick. They were all born on the same astral symbol: Capricorn. Undecided on who was their truest leader, the three of them usually sided with Grenique.

"Uh no, I don't want anything right now," Yogita spoke to a waitress who goolied up to the table and just said the howdy doo. But Yogita was in a trance and wasn't paying attention to anything; she was just moving her rot and making words. The cheena was in a sneety about ancient healing techniques that her and her spiritual sisters shared with one another during their Neteru Council meetings. She was looking at her rooker and remembering that there were nerve and energy meridians at her thumb and fingertips. The meridians contain a nerve energy that works into the body for healing purposes.

Yogita suddenly realized that she hasn't heard a thing on Grenique's whereabouts since the scene of the crast and that was Friday when they had their last meeting on the breathing techniques produced by the Divine Energy. As Grenique was missing in action, she was also holding all the money too and the girls wanted their share of the cutter.

The waitress's litso looked puzzled at Yogita as she was govoreeting with herself inside this half-run down shack of a restaurant. It was called Big Zoobies and all the lewdies in the district went there because the place fixed their firegold real strong at the bar.

"Excuse me, but you can't just sit here and not order anything." said the waitress. She resembled a molody rockstar cheena with her luscious glory died purple and her pale skinny frame. Unlike Yogita this cheena was all legs and stood at least five-nine. Yogita stood just two inches over five feet.

"Oh I am sorry, I will have a white-fish sandwich," she answered the waitress while coming to her senses, "and oh do you have egg-nog?"

"I'll check for ya," the waitress wrote the order on a white notepad and goolied away.

But Yogita shouldn't feel like she'd have anything to worry about. After-all she was wearing her lucky out-fit and her spirits were high anyway. She wore a red spandex top with only one shoulder strap and narrow horizontal splits revealing a peek at her cleavage. The jeans were cut so low that you could see her tattoo of the Egyptian Anhk. Another tattoo of the rebirth symbol Khepera was debuting on her chest. This night it was clear that she didn't have a bra on. Her groodies had perks at the ends in this small top that she was wearing. Looking this way would surely get her into some trouble for the evening.

Yogita's mind was always on sex. You could hear her saying, "white trash sex is the best fuck ever." The other cheenas would simply roll their eyes at her interest in the Anglo-Vecks. They just couldn't pony how a woman could include herself among the Yamassee Nuwaubians, but then submit herself sexually to the enemy at the same time.

Deep into her own daydreaming, Yogita was suddenly distracted from a paper that came falling off the edge of her noga and landed onto the floor near the table where she was sitting. A young lady had dropped it.

"Excuse me you dropped something," Yogita said to the woman then got up from the table and handed the glossy paper to the stranger which appeared to have photos of half-naked women on them.

"Oh thanks!" the girl shouted brightly. Yogita's litso smirked with embarrassment at the bare nagoy groodies in the photo.

"Hey, you smot familiar," said the girl.

"Oh, I am not from this parish," Yogita lied remembering: *never give up your identity to strangers. You never know which party they belong to.*

"Are you sure, I swear I viddy you somewhere before?" the cheena insisted.

"Oh I just moved here from town-down," Yogita lied again knowing damn well she was raised in the lower parishes.

"Oh really, where in town-down?"

"K-2."

"K-2, I though you said you was from the lower parishes. Over in K-2 that's near the Loop?" the girl's litso frowned at Yogita.

Not knowing what to say next, Yogita's goobers clamped hard shut. Thoughts of being raised by a divorced Anglo-Veck foster mother ran wild. She just remembered that she hadn't spoken to her adopted mother in a year, from which she received her last name Pitt since her divorced adopted mother changed back to her old maiden name. Her blood began to race fast and her temples began to throb. What if this girl was with *them*, and had followed her to kill her right now. What would they tell her foster mother if she died today? The only real family that she ever had was her foster mother up until she met up with the council. Maybe they'd say she joined a cult. Maybe they'd tell her foster mother the truth and that Yogita was a washed up thief with varying drug problems, a murderer at that.

"You mean the K-2 near the Loop, I know there's another one besides B-Loop?" the stranger added in. Yogita's rassoodock was in a blank.

"Uuhhh....yyeeaaa...yes! Yes! I am from K-2 near the Loop!" she gathered quickly in order to avoid suspicion.

"Why do you ask?" Yogita was growing deceitful and remembered that she didn't have her gun with her. She also remembered that the reason why she hadn't called Grenique was because she had some of the money that Sheila told her to hide. But now Yogita couldn't remember where she hid the money. They were initially going to lie to Grenique and say that they hadn't gotten any money; this way Grenique would be stupid to give them more cutter. The good thing was that nobody knew how much cutter was actually in the stash. This worried Yogita even more because she knew how greedy Grenique could be. The whole thing happened so fast. They were thrown money in the auto-tron. Nobody counted it. There wasn't anytime to think anything through. Once the rozzers were shot and killed in the hallway of the apartment building, everything else went blank.

"Oh wait a minoota," Yogita said just before the strange girl was about to say something. She moved fast in the direction of the waitress delivering her fish sandwich accompanied by a white tass.

"I have your egg-nog," the waitress said.

"Horrorshow!" Yogita replied. She sat down to eat and could see at the side of her eyes that the strange cheena with all her frizzy hair near the entrance way was walking over towards the booth. Yogita tensed.

"Hey, my name is Cecily are you a dancer?" she asked. She sat down at the booth across from Yogita in a way as if she was inviting herself to do this.

"No, why does everybody keep asking me that….do I really smot like a dancer?" Yogita tried not to govoreet with her rot full but she was so hungry. She looked into a nearby mirror and could see bits of food disgustingly dropping from her rot.

"Well yea, you do."

"No I don't, dancers are super-skinny."

"Not all of them." Cecily insisted.

"Thanks." Yogita replied unsure of the stranger.

"Well I have something that might interest you." Cecily said while passing over the same glossy paper that Yogita picked up for her just a minute ago. Cecily was a mulatto looking ptitsa with high cheekbones and thunderous hips. A light-skinned Negro-Veck cheena, she never felt like she fit in to society. She especially hated when someone described that they could almost viddy her veins because she was so light. Plus, she had a round high-riding ass in the back that she loathed especially when the vecks in the streets cattle-called her. Even the Anglo-Vecks that she briefly dated were more interested in the taboo of the Black side of her. The very tight-sleeveless, tailored top she wore followed the thick curves of her torso and groodies.

"Oh I am sorry, I am not into this," Yogita said while glancing at the half-naked women in the photo, now seeing that it is actually a flier for some nearby strip club. Big glossy florescent colored letters positioned top-center of the cardstock spelled *BREAKTIME*.

"Not into what?" Cecily asked.

"What is this a strip-club?"

"Of course, don't tell me that you are ashamed of your plott." Cecily said while teasing her luscious glory in a nearby mirror. She went to retrieve something from her purse.

"Yea, I don't know if I have the right shape for nagoy dancing," declined Yogita.

"Sure you do, listen I will give you my v-card and you can give me a call. I am not going to convince you to say yes right now. But you can spread a lot of cutter for it. The easiest money you will ever make."

"Really," Yogita's glazzies widened all of a sudden.

"Yup, make at least two grand a week, sometimes you can make that in one nochy." Cecily made it seem like it was no big deal to make all that much money.

"Nothing but big timers come up in Breaktime." She added. While Cecily was so busy jabbing away at her rot, Yogita smotted around for the waitress and seeing that the coast was clear she then pulled out a bottle of Hennessy and poured it into the tass with the egg-nog in it.

"Ohw girl is that some Cognac I am smelling?" Cecily asked.

"Shhh, yea, don't govoreet too loudly about it and tell the whole world," warned Yogita. Judging by the hungry glazzies of Cecily as she watched the direction of the bottle supposed that she may be an alcoholic too. Yogita pushes the tass across the table.

"Here take a sip of the cal, why don't cha….go on." Yogita offered.

Cecily's litso split into a goopy old grin, she almost seemed a bit magoo looking for a second. She placed the edge of the tass to her goobers and sucked down the beige colored liquid. She then let out a roar as her rot opened up yawning like and said:

"Aaagghhh…egg-nog and cognac, now bitch that's some shit!" Her long red polished nails made clicking sounds against the glass and table as she set the tass down.

"Don't worry I think I have a malenky bit more." Yogita laughed. She then spotted something quite familiar on her new friends rooker. It was a tattoo that matched hers.

"Wait let me viddy that." Yogita blurted.

"Viddy what?"

Yogita pointed to the designs on her arm, "this is an Egyptian God."

"It's Kemet, we don't call it Egypt," Cecily corrected, "this is Osiris."

Yogita pulled down the slit in her cleavage area, "you viddy?"

"Mmm...oh that's Khepera," Cecily said while staring at the tattoos on Yogita's groodies. She was a bit impressed with the outcome of the designs.

"It's the scarab beetle," Yogita declared.

"Right. The scarab beetle of Khepera, same cal!" Cecily passed the tass back to Yogita, "thanks for the firegold."

There was silence for a minute as Yogita gave her a nod of approval then proceeded to take another bite of her sandwich.

"Oh wait now I remember where I viddied you once before. Aren't you a member of the YN? I think I viddied you at the Nuwaubian Order meeting that they have." Cecily said.

"Yes I am of the Yamassee, you know they just opened up The Grand Lodge out near the Mayadunna." Yogita said.

"Right, I remember they were renovating some of the buildings out there. Some of the lewdies were govoreeting about how they heard that the Honorable Gerard Basquiat was smotting at property over there. Well they finally did it huh. Wow the Masselmaun have come so far haven't we."

"Yup, they did." Yogita didn't want to be too obvious that the discussion was taking longer than she would have liked. She was waiting for the young woman to get a clue and leave. But the girl just kept on talking. All the while she just remembered that her friend Jason who she was initially supposed to meet for dinner at the restaurant never showed up. Jason was an Anglo-Veck that she met through a mutual friend. They were going to have dinner and then go out and play pool with some friends. Yogita had already been waiting for at least an hour by now and wondered if she should just leave.

"So tell me something....are you really from K-2?"

"What, they don't have lewdies that smot like me in K-2 or something?" Yogita answered with another question.

"No it's not that....I just." Cecily paused.

Yogita laughed suddenly, "As you can viddy I have a problem govoreeting with total strangers."

"Oh no I can pony this...and I don't blame you. You never know what lewdies are up to these days. Gotta watch yur back ya know."

Yogita shrugged.

CHAPTER 7

A few hours had passed into the night and Grenique woke up to find that Lord Perrineau Basquiat had left. She must have slept for hours and her loins were sore from earlier. The room was a mess. Platties were thrown all over the place and table fixtures had been knocked off her nightstand. Grenique sighed from tiredness and didn't have any motive to clean up. She sat down at the edge of the bed and viddied what appeared to be broken pieces of pottery that was scattered all over the floor.

"Oh no my Kerma beaker is broken," she gasped. Tears began to well in her glazzies as she knelt down to the floor. The Kerma beaker was a type of an African ceramic which had been passed down from her grandmother to her mother and was more than a century old. Her grandmother, now deceased, was a survivor of the massacres in Darfur brought on by the *Janjaweed* militias. A victim of rape, she was six months pregnant with Grenique's mother and ready to deliver when she arrived in Droghega more than fifty years ago as a refugee of the Dinka tribe and settled there. Because of the aftermath of the C-11 women were mysteriously giving birth to full born children within six months. There was a drastic environmental shift response after the colossal impact of the C-11 that drowned more than 77 percent of North America. Days were longer and shorter at odd times than usual. Temperatures rose above exceedingly hot levels, but then simmered down thankfully. The weather became more and more complicated to predict. Oddly enough the impact of the C-11 decades ago was to blame for the way people could hear things. Many complained that their hearing was odd and overtime it changed the way people heard English. The English language was compromised and was becoming lost. Natural disasters were, although at a minimum, even still capable of sudden eruption.

Grenique gathered up pieces of the broken Kerma pottery on the floor. She suddenly lapses in and out of flashbacks of the memories her mother shared with her about her grandmother's stories of Sudan. She remembers the horrifying details of Dinka women being raped and the villages being burned down; the many children dying from starvation and how all of this was genocide of the Nilotic people ordained by the Khartoum government. Grenique thinks on her life in Menap and how she was raised by a single mother who was given the name Josephine Bakhita Yousef—named after a Sudanese woman who was famously canonized as a saint by Pope John Paul II. Her struggling mother who worked as a cleaning lady and raised Grenique in the lower district where she witnessed murders against the rival gangs of the *Western Addition Scally Boys* over gang turf and control over the drug dealing particularly surrounding the area.

Grenique's mother Josephine died two years ago from

breast cancer and never knew her father just like Grenique never got a chance to meet her biological father either. All Josephine could remember her mother telling her was that her father was an Egyptian Arab named Hazem Yousef who loved the Dinka.

Grenique's mind raced. She thought on how much time she had to live. After-all she is leading a pretty dangerous life herself so-to-speak. The pitfalls of the low-class dealings of the environment within her upbringing are solely to blame. From the pains of growing up an only child many times she felt lonely. Her desire was to fit in and be the head over everybody. She despised being inconsequential. As long as she was in or about the conversation, she was happy. The center of attention was her goal at most. Grenique had no true family to call her own except her girls in the sorority. The Nuwabians have been her family, her clan for the past four years. All she ever knew about her true father was that he was a descendant of an Old World Indian warrior named John Horse thus how she got her last name. The position of her being a Goddess of the Floating Fortress was through her faith in Nuwaubu and her belief of the Angels from a far away planet called *Proximus Centauri II* who summoned these names for her in a series of oracles. Basically it is some foolish identity that she made up for her own self to be called as people from this group often did. Last she heard about her father was that he disappeared like the land where the state of Florida once was many years ago.

Grenique's tears drop heavily upon the half-broken sketching of St. Josephine Bakhita's litso which was engraved at the center of this black and red polished ceramic. She rubs her fingers against the deep etchings, feeling the designs once more as she just remembered that she had an empty shoebox in the closet. Within moments Grenique pushes open a door and retrieves an empty pink square box from a nearby closet. Carefully, she pours broken pieces of the precious ceramic into the box in hopes of gluing the Kerma beaker back together later.

"Yieth! Oh Yieth…spirits of the Dinka ancestors. I summon protection of Jak to accomplish the task of reversing the curse that seeks to harm me!" She prayed aloud. Suddenly she feels threatened by something. Maybe the breaking of a precious heirloom such as the Kerma beaker was bad luck, a sign of demise. Women didn't appear to live long in her family it seemed. Grenique felt the need to call upon these ancestral spirits to carry her, surround her with reassurance that everything would be okay. The gods knew that this African ceramic meant so much, why would they take it from her?

"Yeahh…yeahh…yeahh Al-Kidr, oh green one, provide me the wisdom through the channels of the ancient moors. Guide me all ye pharaohs of Kemet and dispel the spite of Kingu." Grenique got up to light incense and pulled out her Bellini carpet as she spoke rituals into the Universe to cleanse herself of any demons. She kneeled down upon the reddish-colored rug and faced her Nubian Nation scroll which hung upon a wall slightly to the left of a corner in her bedroom. Near it was placed a brilliant painting of the sphinx which was framed in black.

"Annunaqi." She takes in a deep breath.

"Annunaqi…Eloheem Nuwaubu."

Grenique repeated her chants over and over and bowed constantly so that her chin nearly touched the rug each time. She was entranced in this formation for quite a long time. Her rookers were positioned in front of her so that her fingers were folded into a prayer's fist.

"I am in the love of the all and all love is in me. I am part of the all and the all is a part of me. I am one with the all and the all is one with me. I can succeed as a part of the all and fail as an individual. I can be all that I wish in the all as long as my wish is to stay in the all. I am never alone. The all is—I am. The all can—I can. The all does—I do."

Over the time that Grenique was heavily in devotion to her meditation, the skies had darkened because dense clouds had formed moments ago. The sound of a loud cracking sound was heard. Thunder had set in and flicks of flash lit up the dark skies. Raindrops fell hard and beat against several okno panes that caused slight banging noises inside her Piotr designed domy.

Grenique was disturbed by a loud banging. The sound came from the living room again. She remembered that the oknos were open in the kitchen and strong winds were probably knocking things over as well. Grenique broke away from her prayer rug hoping nothing else had broken as she went to see what the loud banging noise was in the other room.

Stepping into the living room Grenique's rot dropped and she let out a rather loud creech.

"AAAAHHH…..MOMMA!" she screamed. Loud thunder sounds roared the skies above. Inside her domy, blood was everywhere on the living room floor as well as smeared on the walls and couch. It appeared to be coming from a bleeding baby lamb that a woman resembling the looks of Josephine Bakhita was holding in front of Grenique.

"Grenique how come you haven't been painting? Remember arts and crafts. What did I tell you?" the woman said. Her goloss crackled from appearing to be extremely old. Her goobers were all *mappy* like too. Her skin was dark black; her luscious glory was short and coarse. Her litso was scarred just in the center of each cheekbone. Gold colored amulets rested upon her left wrist.

"My child you disappoint me. All of your gifts and you don't even utilize any of them," the strange lady spoke again. She appeared to have the same identity of Grenique's dead mother. The same look in her glazzies and the way she wore her *jalabiya* was the identical imprint of her mother Josephine except that her white *tobe* was now smeared in blood from the dead baby lamb she held. Her feet were bare, but covered in blood also. Her long tobe was cut and ripped in a few places. White powder was smeared along her skin in reverence of mourning for the dead lamb.

All the while that she was praying to the gods, Grenique realized that she somehow must have summoned an ancestral oracle through the spirit realm beholding her very own deceased mother. It was indeed Josephine Bakhita brought back from the dead. The sky blackened more and loud cracks of thunder roared deep from outside the condo. Sheet lightning flashed in bursts of distant light bouncing off tree branches. The flashes distorted the outlining reflections of Josephine's litso. Her litso appeared in and out of focus which left Grenique stunned.

But in her rassoodock not only was Grenique in shock, she was disappointed. Her prayers were a mere gesture to the survival of her Nuwabian community, not a summoning for the gods to send an ancestral oracle by the *lakou*. This was betrayal, it was vodoun even. Who was controlling this? Indeed it was *hounfar* to blame. But who was the responsible *houngan*? Indeed within vodoun society there were no accidents. Someone had sent a vicious spell in the form of Grenique's mother to haunt her dreams.

"Who would do this to me?" Grenique cried aloud. The palms of her hands reach toward her gulliver and she clutches a fist with a handful of luscious glory, tugging it out in frustration.

"SOMEONE PUT VOODOO ON ME!!"

"AHHH!"

"SOMEBODY PUT A SPELL ON ME!"

She twirled her rookers in the air wildly as though to ward off any lethal medium that could be trying to enter her plott. Her cheeks blanched and her glazzies reddened. The expression on her litso became horribly distorted and her plott began to tremble.

Lord Perrineau was driving his Aston Martin down DS-100 near the P-Lane area of the city as he just left Grenique's home a short while ago. He left his Maserati Cambiocorsa back at the house in order to erase any traces on him. He was dressed in his long grey Visigoth styled maxi coat with a bandanna tight around his gulliver. The lord's nerves were unsettled as Candy Lee sat in the passenger seat. He had just picked her up to do a job for him. The Gray Pigs had been acting rather strange lately, possibly from his meeting with Luciano about the *job*. Perri had to keep a low profile which was the real reason about why he went to Grenique's house in the first place. Not only is Grenique a member of the Neteru Council, she is also First Queen to Lord Perrineau in the society of the Bizango although she denies this and sometimes wants to do away with the lord altogether. She just doesn't want to be married, at least not into Polygamy. Lord Perrineau was already married to several other women within the society. Grenique just wasn't sure of this marriage connection. She heard a lot about the forced marriages and sexual abuse. Some of the girls in the Nuwabian community weren't of legal age for consensual sex with an adult. There were even accusations of incest. She often would confess to him that she is tired of running, hiding and dodging all the dodgers. Sometimes the lord had too much weight to share with Grenique and it oftentimes became too much to handle since she had her own affairs to deal with. This was the basis of their many arguments and neither would let down. It was the sex that had them bound tight and the obligation of her role as First Queen to the lord within the society. Before the ceremony would take place Grenique would have to be moved up to Second Queen in preparation of the actual marriage where she is moved up again as Third Queen. Only the Third Queen is recognized as a wife. The first and second queens are seen as lower leveled concubines. This transition has no particular timeline. It varies by caste, family traditions or even how much money can be put forth to literally purchase the wife that you want.

Lord Perrineau's car was a shiny silver and a V8 Vantage Le Mans votron. The best of its kind since only 40 of them were made. The sports car was the only Aston Martin ever sold with the *Le Mans* labeling. Lord Perrineau has many different votrons, not to mention the hottest clothes and the baddest bitches in Menap. He loves those bandannas and so do all the cheenas. Lord Perrineau, or Perri as Grenique often refers to him, is known as tough within the Nuwabian community. His lifestyle and image could produce no other alternative for he is a Basquiat and an heir to the Bizango throne. Image had its importance. Within the Bizango society that upholds the law of Nuwaubu, Lord Perrineau carries the position of Second Prince. His brother Sterling Basquiat, Grand Duke of Mayadunna, is First Prince and will seed the throne upon the passing of their father Gerard.

Gerard Basquiat is an emperor among the Bizango society in Menap and has fifteen children from six wives. Out of the fifteen children there were only seven boys, two of them were murdered allegedly by the Gray Pigs— another secret society that is a rival of the Bizango society. So now there are five young sons who are eligible to take the throne. Perri is second eldest with one older brother Sterling Basquiat ahead of him to seed the throne. Perri's three younger brothers are often referred to as *the other lords* and the sisters can only marry within the Bizango and must have the blessing of the emperor. Men can marry outside of the Bizango as long as women aren't Gray Pigs, but there can be some exception to the rule as long as she denounces any further dealings with the rival societies. Interracial dating is highly discouraged among the members and isn't tolerated although some members do it anyway.

The Bizango, which the name means council of voodoo priests, was formed by three drug kingpins of Menap many years ago. One of the party's founders, a molodoy street thug named Gerard Basquiat grew up having his mind set on getting out of abject poverty. Fast money, fast cars, hot cheenas and big domy's were his goal sets. Soon the gang had 15 other members some who were formally recruited from *The Loop Boys*. These chellovecks all had their aspirations set in the same direction—fast money and women. The Loop Boys already had a reputation around the districts and soon more followers would come. Once the new recruits were initiated, they were obligated to pay entry fees known as "the dues." Requiring the recruits to shed blood of the enemy was termed—"Blood-In" and showed loyalty. But the only way a member could leave the gang was through natural death or death by the hands of the gang termed—"Blood-Out." The color code of their choice by The Loop Boys at the time was red and members of the Bizango party adopted the colors. Ironically The Gray Pigs wore blue, but they were just a chapter and not as well organized. As time went on, members of both gangs grew more fashionable as competition through money laundering, drug pushing, dogfighting, sex trafficking, robberies and constant recruiting of young Negro-Vecks with nothing else to turn to came into place and brought forth a larger capitol. The Bizango soon outnumbered their rivals and set their conquest in place.

Pressured by the position of his father, Lord Perrineau feels that he needs to carry on the tradition of being a leader. But at the same time, while the lord is known as a tough no shit taking prince of dope pushers, the inner soul of him is going through a crisis. Sometimes he thinks about running away and getting out of the dope business all together. Start afresh and seek out a new life beyond the crime ridden streets he's spent most of his life on. He and Grenique have talked about it before, but then he just brushes it off as nonsense govoreeting. As much as he might want to get out, the life has got him in a death grip.

Lord Perrineau pulls out a cancer stick from his carman.

"Say baby you got a light?" the lord asks while positioning the unlit cancer stick between his goobers. Candy Lee passes him a shiny red lighter that she retrieved from her purse. Up ahead traffic was slow moving and Perri was growing inpatient.

"Move bitch, get out the way!" he screeches at the other auto-trons.

Candy Lee sees something odd about the traffic up ahead, "what is that over there?"

Her glazzies are fixated toward what looks like a crowd of people fighting one another.

"Hell if I know, but we are bout to be late and I can't miss this deal!" Perri begins to push on the car horn.

"Look, you're going to have to get out and walk Candy."

"Bullshit!" she exclaimed. "I ain't gettin' out and walkin' nowhere! Are you crazy. I got five inch heels on."

"Welly-well-on get out and walk, it ain't that far and make sure you count all the money!"

"Fuck you asshole, I ain't gettin' out and walkin' nowhere for nobody....what's up with your welly-well-on!"

Just as Lord Perrineau was about to raise his right rooker and slap Candy's litso with it, a series of rather large explosions were heard sending the two of them into a state of shock.

"What in the hell was all that cal," Candy gasped.

The explosions sent a mass of fireballs, burning debris and noxious fumes skyward. Screeches of the lewdies around them could be heard as many of them ran into the streets and away from the burning buildings.

"We gotta get outta here!" The lord pulls the votron

into reverse, but there are newly abandoned auto-trons surrounding them in a jam-packed sort of way as people ditch their vehicles in efforts of running to safety.

"GET OUT!!" The lord screeches as he presses the door ajar emergency button. The car doors swing open instantly. Just as a large fireball races toward them, the two of them ditch the vehicle just in time.

CHAPTER 8

saac and Gary are driving towards the B-Loop. They just left the scene of the crast a couple minutes ago at Sheila's place.

"Aww shit man I left my calling screen at that bitch's domy!" Gary yelled.

"So what forget that phone man, get another one!" Isaac yelled back while driving.

"I don't want another one okay mutherfucker!"

"Shut the fuck up, you always bitchin' bout something."

"Man look I will knock you the fuck out!"

"Do it then!" Isaac positions his litso as if ready to get hit by Gary but he does nothing.

"I didn't think so. Now shut the hell up!"

Gary begins to chuckle a bit.

"What's so funny?" Isaac asks.

"Nothing man."

"Nawh man tell me what's so funny!" Isaac demands.

"Its just that....well you putting on some pounds man. It ain't like you to fall behind like that and all. I mean you could barely keep up. I thought I was for sure going to lose you after we left that bitch's domy."

"Aww the hell with you man, I ain't puttin' on no pounds, that's yo momma puttin' on the pounds bro." Isaac returned.

"Whatever!"

"Yea, whatever my ass."

"I am just saying I don't wanna hang out with no blimp."

"Oh now I am a blimp."

Gary feels tense suddenly as he realizes that Isaac is slowly pulling the auto-tron to a stop.

"Ay man what are you doing?" Gary asks sensing that he probably said something to really put his partner in a bad mood.

"I am hungry, let's get something to eat up here." Isaac said while pulling the vehicle into the parking area of a taco and burger joint.

Moments later the two are sitting down outside on a bench enjoying a few tacos and burgers that they just ordered.

"You think they know?" Gary asks Isaac a question with a rot full of food.

"Know what?"

"You know, bout me running with the Gray Pigs."

"So what if they know, you with us now, forget them." Isaac assured.

"Yea, those Loop Boys ain't nothin' but a bunch of pussies anyway. I am glad I left them behind. They are just too unorganized." Gary complained.

"Right, like I said they are history. We are in control as we have always been bro. Don't even sweat it."

"You know what's so messed up about them. They shot an old cheena just for cutting in front of them. And a little kid too. Like they thought he was going to tell the cops or something. They don't care."

"That's messed up bro." Isaac frowned.

"Can you believe it, a little two year old boy, shot dead in the head. I tell you what though, we gotta watch out for Lord Perrineau and his droogs." Gary said. His glazzies showed a bit of uneasiness all of sudden.

"Yo we gotta get Leroy out as soon as we can." Isaac said changing the subject.

"I heard he got caught, I didn't want to believe it. That night was crazy."

"It was Lord Perrineau that set that shit up too. You know Grenique is his cheena.

She'd do anything for his ass, including killing us."

"Yea lewdies like that are nuts, they don't think and they don't care who gets hurt."

"I don't know man this is some tricky cal that we are in." Isaac said.

"So what it ain't like we don't have any pooshkas of our own."

"Ey, we play it smart. Don't go flashing all the pooshkas around."

Inside a dingy room in a studio apartment Gary Overdrawn sweats heavily from anxiety while sitting on the edge of a wooden chair. He counts his half of the cutter stolen from Sheila's house that he split with Isaac earlier. His glazzies show worry. Sheila Foxtail was left for dead. He remembers Isaac choking her real horrorshow. Gary stares up at a picture of the Saint Josephine Bahkita that is fixated along a wall. Pulling his shades, he strips to the nagoy and kneels down to the floor. Looking down, he examined the spiked pain belt clamped around his thigh. All true followers of The Way wore this device—a leather strap, studded with sharp metal barbs that cut into the flesh as a perpetual reminder of Saint Josephine Bahkita's suffering. She was the patron saint of Africa. He removes the belt from his thigh in order to keep from gaining any infection. The pain belt shouldn't be worn for more than two hours.

"Ewshff," Gary winced in pain. The metal barbs were beginning to be too much. His body recoiled. Earlier he was a monster as he grasped the buckle pulling it one whole notch tighter. This was his way of savoring the cleansing ritual of pain and suffering.

Pain is good, Gary whispered, repeating the sacred mantra of Father Malachi Z. York—the Master of all Masters. Although York had disappeared without a trace some fifteen years ago, his teachings lived on. Some feared him dead at this point as rumors were at large that he was murdered at the hands of the Black Rosicrucians, a deadly sect that hated the Nuwabian Moors. The Black Rosicrucians were even more deadly than the Janjaweed Militia. Yet the wisdom of Father York lived on, his words still spoken among millions of faithful servants within the Mayadunna and performed the sacred practice known as the Ancient and Mystic Order of Malichizodok.

"Annunaqi." He takes in a deep breath and paces the wooden floor.

"Annunaqi…Eloheem Nuwaubu." Gary chants more and more.

"Yeahh…yeahh…yeahh Al-Kidr, oh green one, provide me the wisdom through the channels of the ancient moors. Guide me all ye Pharaohs of Kemet and dispel the spite of Kingu." Gary got up to light incense and pulled out his Bellini carpet as he spoke rituals into the Universe to cleanse himself of any demons. He knelt down upon the reddish-colored rug and faced his Nubian Nation scroll which hung upon a wall slightly to the left of a corner in his bedroom. Near it was placed a brilliant painting of the sphinx which was framed in black. Gary repeated his chants over and over and bowed constantly so that his chin nearly touched the rug each time. He was entranced in this formation for quite a long time. His rookers were positioned in front of him so that his fingers were folded into a prayer's fist.

"I am in the love of the all and all love is in me. I am part of the all and the all is a part of me. I am one with the all and the all is one with me. I can succeed as a part of the all and fail as an individual. I can be all that I wish in the all as long as my wish is to stay in the all. I am never alone. The all is—I am. The all can—I can. The all does—I do."

These very rituals are what he used as an escape as all Brotherhood experienced, but still the memories haunted his soul. Gary would command himself to forgive those who trespassed. But he was such the hypocrite too as well. More oftentimes he was the transgressor. The memories of purgatory came as always when he least expected it. The memories of the barry which had been his world for seven years and memories of urine and feces, the cries of the hopeless and forgotten prestoopnik bugged him repeatedly.

Gary was forced out of the domy by an evil stepfather at the age of thirteen. His mother simply couldn't do anything since she was pregnant with their fourth child and Gary was the oldest. Money was tight and since there usually wasn't any cutter to spread; there simply wasn't enough love to go around either. His stepfather who was an unemployed drunk, a burly carpenter by trade that grew increasingly enraged by the thought of having another rot to feed, beat his mother regularly although he gave her a break at one point in time since she was visibly pregnant. Whenever Gary would try to intervene, he too was badly beaten. Some months later Gary would learn that his pregnant mother just shy of her delivery was murdered by her husband who then turned the revolver on himself and blew off his head. Her fetus never survived as she was shot in the stomach.

In the barry for seven years for armed robbery, among other crimes that were thrown at him, Gary was introduced to the Nuwaubian Army. Before he found The Brotherhood, or them finding him since the twenty-five-year old really had no other alternative in prison, Gary would oftentimes blame himself for his mother's death. But now that he had a family again he no longer blamed himself. As a young child growing up in the lower parishes of Hunts People, which was known as a gang infested area of District 7 he found it equally impossible to find any comfort. His odd behavior and appearance made him an outcast among the other runaways and he was forced to live alone in a dilapidated warehouse, eating stolen bread and raw fish. His only comfort was that in ragged newspapers and magazines known as gazettas, or "brainwashing papers" as some lewdies called it.

"Give it back to me!" A young Gary no more than seven

years old screams back at another youth two years older than him. Another drifter Tommie mocked Gary on the streets and always attempted to steal his food. After days went by and Gary couldn't take it any longer, the young kid found himself pummeled near to his death. At the age of nineteen, while attempting to steal a loaf of bread from a local corner store Gary was caught by the store owner's brother. Gary slammed into the guy causing him to trip sideways over the railing. The force of the slamming then caused him to bang his head into a side window which burst open. Shards of glass cut open his skin and blood poured all over the floor. The store owner was able to grab the arms of Gary and together they locked into severe fighting. The millicent came just in time from a tip by several bystanders and Gary was arrested. He was sentenced ninety days in the Staja.

The memories of abandonment surfaced enormously and filled Gary's tick-tocker with hatred. This is why he joined up with the teaching of Issa Al Haadi Al Mahdi. Long before Manep, Al Mahdi was the inventor of the quasi Muslim Black nationalist movement in the old world. As Al Mahdi started the Ansaar Pure Sufi ministry to a group who called themselves Nubians in Brooklyn, New York back in 1967 the group later grew reputation among followers as the Black Hebrews phenomenon. By 1969 the group had enough followers to begin what was dubbed The Nubian Hebrew Mission and chapters sprung up across the United States as Al Mahdi conducted his tours.

In 1970 Al Mahdi went to a pilgrimage in Egypt where he gave his devotion to the Great Temple of Abydos. It was there where Al Mahdi met with the true Nubians of Africa and was formally introduced to the Science of Nubianism which later transformed back here in many ways during the Drogheda Period of 2050 as did the Science of Nuwabianism to his followers. Later on the Nuwabian Nation of Moors would presume itself into existence and spread through many chapters growing into a population of over six million in counting. Some presumed maybe even more.

The term Nubian was founded among the Africans living in Sudan, a country located just south of Egypt. The Sudanese were outcasts to the Egyptians and were made into slaves. This dated back as early as 1700 B.C. Over time the Sudanese Nubians shifted where most modern Nubians would claim to be Arabic. The influx of Arabs migrating south from Egypt to Sudan had contributed to the loss of the Nubian identity following the collapse of the last Nubian kingdom around 1504. In modern times Nuwabianism simply evolved from the derivative of the New Nubian label in conjunction with the historical artifacts brought on by Islamic Mysticism of Egyptian Moors. The term Moor itself was the classical term by Europeans describing North African Muslims later on. However, the New Order of Manep was trying to get the followers within the Mayadunna to erase their past. The New Order was the threat. Gerard Basquiat saw to it that their history was preserved and past down generations despite this new order—the Nuwabi, the Bizango, the Mayadunna they were all connected. They were all one family under one Islamic Nubia no matter their inner turmoil.

A little time had passed and Gary awoke from his mattress. He had no idea what awoken him or how long he had been sleeping. *Was I dreaming?* He slowly began to rise from the frameless mattress that unevenly sat upon its box spring. Whispering which came from the hallway behind the closed front door disrupted the stillness of the air. Gary felt an unexpected wariness suddenly.

Standing and wearing only a pair of boxers, Gary tip-toed over to the window. *Was I followed?* As he looked around he couldn't see anything out of the usual, in fact the blue bicycle was still locked up to a poll in the same way he saw it when he first got home and several children played jump rope near a fire hydrant. He listened. Silence. *What's got me so uneasy?* Gary taught himself to pay attention to his own intuition. At an early age it was all he could rely on. Intuition was what kept him alive on the streets as a child long before prison. A floorboard creaked just outside the front door in the hallway. Peering out the okno, Gary now viddied the faint outline of a millicent vehicle. But then a sound could be heard at the front door as the latch moved suddenly.

Just before the door burst open, Gary dashed across the room and slid to a stop in front of it. A millicent officer stormed through swinging his pooshka-filled rookers from left to right in what at first appeared to be an unoccupied room. In an instant, Gary shoved his shoulder into the door, slamming the officer's gulliver into the siding which in turn caused the officer to drop his weapon. The blasting sound of a pooshka startled Gary as he realized that there was another millicent officer behind the first one. A series of pooshka firing ensued and blood splattered along the front entrance.

Gary hurriedly got himself dressed and hurled his body down the staircase. *Someone betrayed me.* He thought to himself, but who was it that ratted him out? When he reached the foyer, more of the millicent was surging through the front door. Gary turned on his heel and split into a different direction dashing deeper into the residence hallway. He now saw the door he sought. *Ah the broken exit light. Go!* Running full speed through the door and out in the street, Gary leapt off the low landing, not seeing the officers coming the other way until it was too late.

CHAPTER 9

nside the millicent department the rozzers turned and moved out onto the street. Captain Warren Clarke watched the police ranks disappear through the doors. At the rear of the room he caught a glimpse of the deputy inspector stepping into an office whose door was marked **"Captain Warren Clarke,"** in chipped lettering.

Inspector Donovan McNabb was well over six-foot and smartly dressed, weighing about two-hundred pounds. He sat with his back to the door. He now turned partially around revealing a handsome, shaven blue-eyed litso. "Nice office ya got here Warren." The only light came from the fluorescent desk lamp and it put his litso in a semi-silhouette. Clarke came to the other side of the desk and looked down into a litso that seemed too molodoy to be that of a deputy inspector. "I must say that was some govoreeting you gave the other day about what's happening out here in Menap." McNabb spoke again.

"You seem surprised," said the captain, faking docility and sitting down opposite him. "Don't you think what happened here the other night called for me to say something as strong as that?"

McNabb looked at Clarke from under a furrowed brow.

"The MS-13 manual has been updated with more realistic viewpoints captain."

"The book is in the process of being re-edited," Clarke erupted back.

"You have to understand the times we live in. Things are continuously changing," said the inspector, "what was practical and right yesterday can be terrible and wrong today. It's a necessity that Our People, the lewdies, no matter what their personal feelings, go along with what is happening."

Warren Clarke had all but stopped listening by now. He had read the memorandums that came down to the local police departments from the burgeoning elite who suddenly seemed to have filled the headquarters.

Menap was experiencing the explosion of narcotics related homicides recently. The millicent chief was called in to administer a task force along with his veteran homicide inspectors to solve and suppress violent illegal narcotics pushers and their cell groups. The operation was termed C.R.U.S.H, an acronym for Crime Response Unit to Suppress Homicides. The task force also teamed up on occasion with Operation TARMAC, a multi-agency unit brought on by Menap Security to track criminals and terrorist groups. The cleverness of these individuals augmented and supported the homicide detail, solving well over 65 murders, making several felony arrests and convictions for violent crimes, scores of seized narcotics and 250 assorted handgun and assault weapons. But recent govoreeting by hopeless lewdies has it that the Menap Millicent Department has been frequently met with criticism, unavoidable due to problems of accountability and corruption that has plagued the department. Another fact is that an investigation brought on by the district's judge found that more than 3 million per year was being secretly pocketed by the officer class from regular payoffs by prostitution and gambling.

At least by now a bottle of whiskey should be put on the table with two shot tasses already emptied by us, McNabb thought to himself. But there was no fraternizing with Clarke. No hanky panky cal. Clarke used the Millicent Department and its civil service examination for stepping stones to success by grabbing notice with his quick rise, his memberships in the right clubs and the appropriate political connection. Having exhausted all levels of testing and climbing to the top so quickly Clarke bonded himself with the proper circle of people within the city administration that were smotting for an imagery to protect. They were the new intellectual party of rozzers and public relations advisers for The New Order.

"Why would or should there for that matter be any difference now in our reaction when two rozzers get killed in the line of duty than it was ten years ago, or even twenty? Aren't we supposed to react to this, or do we have a new fucking code to go by that I don't know anything about?" Clarke said as he leaned across the desk. His heavy rookers folded in front of him.

McNabb's glazzies burst with signs of consternation at Clarke. He had no answers for the moment. His past experiences proved that at his rank and presence he was certainly able to convince department commanders to anxious nods of approval about most things he said, especially when they had trouble. He seemed intrigued by Clarke's candid rebuttals.

"Circumstances, well let's just say that they are, or should be, examined a little more carefully now. Besides"— McNabb's smile broadened as if he were dismissing the question with a forced sense of good fellowship—"that's the way the department wants it so who are we to argue with it, huh, Captain?"

The complacency of McNabb's condescending answer persuaded Clarke into deeper discussion. "Well, then, don't you think it's about time we started to ask some questions Detective?"

"Come on, Clarke. You govoreet as if you don't read the gazettas! What about the memorandums and reports coming out of headquarters?" McNabb didn't raise his goloss but was stern in his speech. He also knew how far not to push the captain.

Clarke's glazzies dropped; his resentment of the deputy inspector and all he stood for was carrying him too far. Twenty-five years of a semi-military life were too deeply ingrained; the rank deserved respect. A brief silence held in the room while Clarke showed a litso full of distaste. When he looked up he felt it safe to govoreet, but indignation seeped through his tone like smoke under a closed door.

"Inspector, forgive me if I seem out of bounds, but if I ran this police department completely by that new book you're referring to, the criminal lewdy would eat us alive. We might as well tear the whole building apart. That's right, burn it down! Because the only semblance to law and order would be the governor sending in the troops to protect the lily Anglo-Veck store owners' interest and us from the snipers."

The captain shifted his weight a bit in the chair. McNabb's glazzies shifted throughout the photos of Captain Clarke's family on a desk while he listened. In one picture was the captain's wife. She was an old bag of a looking woman as her goobers were all mappy. Her litso was quite peeled. Pictures of his sons and daughters also with their children and spouses showed depressing upturned litsos and they all wore black koshtooms. They each wore a pin designed with the seal of The Bones and Skulls Fraternal Order on the upper left part of their shirts. This pin was a symbol of acceptance by The Family and was worn most of the time but not always. It was the one with the Red Lodge symbol.

"You sloosh, I am only going to give it to you straight. I am talking about the underworld element, The Party!"

"Shit we have to deal with everyday." McNabb jumped in.

"Yea, a malenky bit more shit that we have to deal with everyday bro. They're the animals who are not going to give us any respect. Not the least bit of it. I tell ya, this new liberal approach to millicent work they govoreet may look fine on paper but they ought to come up here and pull ten to twelve hours per day. I think there glazzies would be opened to viddy what we are all up against."

McNabb's glazzies wandered a bit more about the room and up to an iron-mesh okno and down again to the filing cabinets pressed up against the walls. Pictures of wanted men, profiles and full shots were tacked up across a black board. McNabb avoided as much as he possibly could on showing his irritation. He detested the captain for copping out behind an apology and then using it as a guise to continue to talk against fresh insights and polices. McNabb had to come to terms with the fact that he was still under the watch from the old guard, those great protectors of the rich class. He was called in to oversee regulations, to give instructions on what to tell the press so they could publish it in the gazetta all while still fighting to protect the imagery of the department.

Clark's indifference to his position has somehow turned McNabb into an illegal interrogator. For the right to have a lawyer present during questioning was so quickly mentioned and so frequently denied, along with the prestoopnik's other rights, then even if Clarke had got what he wanted McNabb doubted the testimony would have stood up in The Party Jury. The deputy inspector just wanted to make it clear that he witnessed the captain's uncalled-for speech, no matter how it was made without clearance. What was called for now was an immediate answer. What seemed to be happening instead was the prodding of policy met with much smoldering sarcasm that split their official relationship in the first place and opened up a huge mess of antagonism being passed back and forth.

"We fully realize Clarke, that there are extenuating circumstances in a number of commands, and as you know, we let each department captain have a certain amount of authorized freedom in judging his own problem area. But sending the rozz out on the street with a **Win-One-For-The-Marionette Man** speech, I've got to consider you a joke, but a very dangerous joke at that. Because I don't think you fully comprehend the trouble you could be inviting for the whole department. Those suits you send out, they don't need govoreeting like this. For a number of years we have been trying to indoctrinate them into a broader understanding of the times and the temper of the districts, and to bring that knowledge into the neighborhoods and ports they patrol. Wouldn't their appearance alone been enough to spread intimidation for tightening up the area? But no you go and juice them up and give them your authorization to go out and bust gullivers open in an indiscriminate display of force that's going to catch a lot of innocent lewdies who are going to get back at you for fucking them with no vaseline! And then maybe we just get a few more militant Negro-Veck organizations parading outside crying brutality by the millicent. Your lack of responsibility has shown, Captain, to the men under your control, to your job and to the community that you are supposed to protect. You can be certain that this is going into my official report."

"Lay them off." Clarke muttered.

"What?"

"Then we can just lay everybody the fuck off then, won't we!" The captain tempered.

"If the millicent were trying to avoid dratsing, why were they the ones encouraging the rivalry between the gangs?" McNabb shouted with fierce. Obviously neither one was listening to each other. They were just stepping over each other's sentences.

"It's convenient captain. We need the gangs to exist, right, captain?" McNabb went on, his goloss in a quiet and manipulating tone. "It's the nature of the business in your rassoodock. Why you would get lots of the pretty polly for it wouldn't ya think? Let's see as long as gangs exist, you're allowed to apply for more millicent and for more money. If gang members don't exist, you lose business. But then when it is all said and done, you go out and scheme between you and your *good ole' boys* for a larger take in the money and then you issue some secret hold out, or in this case, fire a bunch of the staff off so that they never get paid for your dirty work!"

Captain Clarke knew that Detective McNabb had been pissed off well past the point of no return, but he didn't care. He was done, dead before he had even walked into the room and now he knows that the deputy inspector is out to do him in. This didn't matter however, because with Clarke's added footnotes on the report and backing from his boys, the report would be judged on the level of contradictory. McNabb's statements were brought on by prejudicial malice and were full of inaccurate allegations.

"Be sure, Detective, that you'd better hope you remember to note down the reasons behind my actions or your papers are useless." The captain's rookers grasped the sides of the chair as if he was about to rise, but he remained seated.

"This is different what took place up here. It's unique. It's different because of the situation surrounding the case. A Menap gang leader loses a lot of the cutter while his droogs are knocked off along with a couple of Anglo-Veck syndicates who happened to be members of a so-called fraternal organization. But then somehow this fraternal organization got themselves mixed up with the involvement of a Negro-Veck, Quasi-Islamic voodoo sect gang who refer to themselves as The Nuwabian Moors and who have a vicious known reputation for being merciless killers. It's the biggest crime to tolchock the city. Islam is a religion of violence and hate and must be stopped, detective. This Nuwabian Moor clan plans to kill more of The millicent. We already lost two patrolmen, McNabb. We cannot afford to lose more. The govoreeting is spread and now Menap is waiting for the backlash, fully expecting us to storm out through the streets in a fit of revenge. I cannot disappoint them. I believe this to be basic police psychology in any lower parish."

Although he didn't believe the gangs were highly organized, or tightly connected with one another in any particular fashion, one thing Clarke knew was that the spiraling gang battles were worse than anything he had seen in his some two decades in with the peacekeepers.

Clarke sprung up from the chair like a chicken pointing his index rooker at a photo of a mugshot on a blackboard. "You see this! These thugs have completely taken over the whole Hunts People section detective in case you didn't know this already. One of them wounded a 2-year-old girl during a vicious gunfight." The captain moved his index rooker down and was pointing at another mugshot photo, "this bastard here was set free just five days after he shot this little girl." Captain Clarke positions his index rooker on a picture of a young black child. In the photo the young black girl dressed in pink smiled ever so bright while holding a doll. "Despite a rap sheet that includes 22 arrests, as well as pending felony charges, the killer was released. He killed her in front of her domy in broad daylight. Sadly this all happened as she unknowingly intercepted the cross firing of two droogs firing at a third thug in revenge for an earlier mugging. This happened to her all while innocently riding her bike in front of her own home, detective. If we don't react with a quick show of strength, especially now in the next few hours, they will begin to suspect that maybe our fight has softened. I am simply saying to you, detective, we lose respect and we lose a lot of any standing edge if we don't respond. It's the two-bit Black bastards with their get rich-quick ideas. It's them to watch out for McNabb. There the ones with the pooshkas stashed away who didn't have the guts to use them before. Now they might just as well start to look around for the stickups because it's easy. They have their army in place."

In an authoritative way the captain was now pointing his index rooker at McNabb's litso. "My first action is to continue doing my job as well as I can and that includes letting the punks and punkettes, the puppets and their droog junkies know right away that the godamn arsenal up here stays!" The deputy inspector had dropped his glazzies toward Clarke's moving rooker, "more important to me is to let the lewdies know that we take pride in our forces," the captain continued.

"Captain, I fear you to be awfully blind, for you can't see past the boundaries of your own corrupt police department!" McNabb retorted.

"Just remember everything that I said before," the captain's goloss sounds high with confidence, "cause if you can't, I would be more than happy to repeat it in person to whoever you hand your report to."

"Again Captain, I don't think you fully realize what charges this can bring. You may not like the system but surprisingly it has worked for a number of years. It doesn't need someone like you to go and try to turn it all around in one night. This is an official order. From here on out we play this thing down until it is said and done. A dead issue with the men working under your control. We don't want this to get out to the Tele-Screen. Because this thing that happened two nights ago could be easily misinterpreted, especially since our statements say it was a local heist of an inconsequential sum. We cannot let it get out to the Tele-Screen that it was a big syndicate crast. It would only make our patrolmen out to be looking as if they were riding shotgun for a large take of blood money."

CHAPTER 10

Yogita Pitt was at the nightclub Breaktime and decided to take up Cecily's offer of seeing what this scene was really all about. The parking lot was full with nothing but expensive mobile pods and auto-trons. Yogita had taken up the ride with Cecily on a whim, but also held up her guard just in case anything out of the ordinary happened later she would be prepared.

Inside, the nightclub was dark and there was one silver pole in the middle of an elevated stage. One would have to pass through big red curtains from the main entrance after successfully passing the door guards. Once in, loud rhythms of r&b and hip-hop music could be heard blasting through huge speakers positioned above the tall walls. Yogita could see that the place was decorated with furniture that oddly represented the female anatomy. A table top had breasts on it and legs shaped like a woman, and the bar cabinets had wooden breasts for handles. The back curtain entrance in the rear of the room was V-shaped like that of a woman's vagina and appeared to be an exit of where the erotic dancers would eventually come from. The tall walls which were all painted red were full of erotic photographs of naked women in suggestive positions. Some were colored photos, but many were in the old-fashioned black and white.

A rush of panic filled the area as a dancer just emerged from behind the red V-shaped curtain. She was a dark-skinned Black cheena, with big groodies. She had a *meat-n-potatoes* backside with a small torso and wore just a bathing suit top and small mini-skirt bottom. She wore jet-black spiked heels too. Immediately she stripped off the top bra and bottom skirt to reveal a pink g-string bikini. The crowd went wild just as soon as she turned around to reveal a rather large derriere. Excited men rushed to the front row of the stage waving dollar bills in their rookers.

Suddenly, Yogita thought she may have viddied a rooker waving at her and then realized that it was Cecily getting her attention to come over to where she was sitting.

"Hey girl," Yogita said aloud over the loud *doobidoob*, but thought to exaggerate her goobers in talking formation so that Cecily could make out what she was govoreeting. As Yogita goolied to the table she noticed that a few other girls were sitting next to her, but then everyone suspiciously got up from the table all at the same time as if this was something pre-planned. Yogita was cautious of everyone's move. Things just didn't seem the same since last Friday night's crast.

As Yogita got closer Cecily quickly grabbed her rooker in an instant and they went over to where a door was opened for them by a big Black man wearing a black suit. The communication device that was clipped to his earlobe was a suggestion that he was security and Yogita felt a little bit more at ease. If anything she could just scream at him for help if anything went too crazy. Besides, Cecily was a sweet girl who didn't seem to mean any harm anyway. *Let your guard down girl.* Yogita thought to herself.

Down a short hallway and a few quick steps to the right, the ladies were all in tow as a shirtless athletic-looking man escorted them into a secluded lounge.

"Oh my gawd, look at him," Cecily quipped. The girls all gasped in unison at the handsome and young medium-sized boy who looked barely of legal age to be inside of any nightclub.

"That's the owner's son." Cecily informed everyone.

"Oh he is so fine!" Yogita said while smiling, "and how old are you."

"Old enough." He responded smartly and goolied off.

"Don't worry about that, he's used to people picking at his cute self," a girl interrupted, "Hi my name is Mariel."

Yogita extends her rooker, "ole' Cecily here is bad at introducing people I guess, hi I am Yogita." They shake rookers.

"We know." The girls laughed but Yogita didn't.

"What's so funny?" Yogita asked.

"Oh nothing, hi my name is Brianna." Another girl introduced herself.

As they sat in the private booth, Yogita noticed that the sound quality in the room cut out a lot of the blaring noises from the speakers so she could hear the girls' voices better.

Shortly after sitting down, another shirtless waiter wearing only a white g-string entered the booth. This one was taller and more ripped with muscles. He was also a bit older, but not much. Just next to the table the waiter's panhandle was hanging firmly dressed by the tip of the g-string in front of Mariel and the cheenas were laughing.

"Awwhh…another fine veck that survived extermination!" Cecily bantered.

"There you go talking about that damn movie again Cec!" Mariel said.

"What movie?" asked Yogita.

"You didn't viddy the movie Marionette Man?" Mariel asked.

"No…uhn-uhn…I didn't. What is it about?" asked Yogita.

"Oh it's kinda like that movie about the Nadsat speakers, but only better and this time it's a lot more Negro-Vecks in it."

"Got that right!" Cecily said while staring at the muscled Black dude in front of her.

"And what can I get you fine cheenas to drink this nochy?" The waiter asked. His goloss had a touch of a noticeable accent.

"A tall tass of you." Mariel snickered. Standing at about 5'8" and weighing approximately 125 pounds she had a perfect dimpled smile to go with all her curves. This cheena had no problem using her good looks to get what she wanted, especially from men.

"I'll have a Godmother Firegold," Cecily said quickly.

"Ooh what's in a Godmother?" Brianna asked.

"Vodka and Amaretto." Cecily replied.

"Oh ya'll ready to get fucked up!" Yogita chimed in.

"Oh yea…yea…we ready. Get me a Hurricane!" Brianna said with cheer while waiving her rookers in the air with excitement. Brianna Rahman was a rare dark-skinned beauty with green eyes that sparked as emeralds. Right now she was living in a two-room shack with her roommate Mariel and was desperate to get out of a bad situation. Not too long ago she was hired by Madame Pavarotti sister of mafia Don Luciano Pavarotti to do work as an escort.

Brianna had just entered *the game* during the first expansion. She wanted something new, something different, something erotic. It wasn't until she met up with Madame Pavarotti that she felt that she reached some sort of conquest. Luckily the Madame was still hiring.

"Mariel and Yogita what y'all havin'?" Cecily asked.

"Pass the Courvoisier!" shouted Yogita in sing-song.

"I am with Yogita on that. Make that a full bottle!" Mariel said with cheer.

A short while had passed and the waiter returned with a small circular server tray full of exotic cocktails and a bottle of Courvoisier. Cecily reached over to Yogita with a twenty-dollar bill, "Here Yogita, give this to him."

The waiter seeing that he was about to get tipped, moved his rookers above his gulliver and gyrated his plott before pushing his groin closer to the bill in Yogita's rooker.

"Put it in his g-string," Cecily leaning over had said in a low tone at Yogita.

As she did this, she saw that the waiter-turned-stripper was glaring with serious glazzies at her.

"Thank you." He said while taking her rooker and kissing the back of it.

"Okay cheenas, its time to take it to the gulliver, come on everyone grab your tasses!" Mariel was proposing a toast.

All together the girls all smashed their tasses together and took several large gulps of drink.

"Ey boy, why don't you give us a hot treat." Cecily said boldly. Yogita figured the alcohol was sort of giving everyone a bit of confidence to ask what they really wanted from the nearly nagoy waiter. Besides he was just standing there anyway hopelessly waiting for something to happen.

"Ya'll want the regular VIP or the Private VIP?" asked the waiter.

"PRIVATE!" The girls all screeched in unison.

"Howz about it. A little doobidoob, yea?" The waiter asked. The man then went over to the door and turned the lock. He started dancing over by Brianna first. Then he made his way around the room while letting each of the girls take turns spanking his butt. He gyrated over to a neon lit screen that was sort of embedded in the wall and touched a series of codes on the touch-screen where the neon lit lettering spelled the words music on it. Within seconds music filled the room and the waiter centered himself while pausing for dramatic purposes. He then ripped off his loin cloth exposing a nude panhandle.

"Oh lawd, have mercy!" Brianna screeched while fanning herself.

"Damn, King Kong!" Cecily yelled too and took another gulp from her cocktail. Soon it was gone. But then she reached over to the bottle of Courvoisier on the table and helped herself by pouring it into her newly emptied tass. The girls were all completely amazed. The man's panhandle was at least twelve inches and it had girth too. It didn't seem real as it just hung there.

This time when King Kong made his way around the

room, it was more sensual as he was now more exposed. He first placed his panhandle in Mariel's rooker, then he moved on over to Cecily and Brianna. Lastly, Yogita copped a feel. By his third trip around the room, he incorporated their plotts into the show. Caressing and sucking on Brianna's groodies through her shirt, until her glazzies closed in ecstasy and her nipples were popping through. Standing Brianna up, he positioned her front towards the black leather sofa and bent her over. As her rookers were placed on the back of the sofa he began mocking the *doggie style* sex position with her. As she remained in that bent-over-position, he stood off to the side of her, reached over to the back of her nogas and began stroking. Slowly up and down. Then side to side he went on her. It marked the first time anyone had been able to shut this girl up all night.

"Uhhh-uhh." Brianna moaned helplessly. After making such passionate noises, Kong really decided to do a number on her. He began to move faster and harder while he stroked her. Her plott began to shiver from the touch. She grabbed his rooker with intense excitement while panting. Her goobers folded and her glazzies rolled back in their sockets.

"Did she just cum?" Yogita asked while pointing at them.

"Sshhh...be quiet!" Cecily stopped Yogita with a quickness. She didn't want any type of spontaneity compromised by any talking out of place. The mood was right for some hot action and the girls all knew this. Cecily aimed to keep it this way. At least for the moment, there was plenty of time for govoreeting later. Yogita just sat in utter shock. She had to take another gulp, this time she grabbed the whole bottle and chugged it down straight.

Mariel couldn't help but giggle at all this. She just knew she would be next, but then she pointed a rooker at Yogita.

"Uhn-Uhn Bitch NO!" Yogita screeched at the concept. She was just too shy at the moment to be handled like that from a total stranger.

"Hold out your rookers baby." Kong demanded of Yogita. As she did what she was told—to her objection of course—Kong had just poured warm oil into her nervously shaking rookers. He then positioned his panhandle in her rookers, while his glazzies signaled for her to begin stroking it.

"Work that magic show em' your skillz Yogita!" Cecily screeched. He began to give Yogita the same treatment that he gave Brianna just a moment ago. He mainly began caressing and nipple pinching Yogita through her top. Then he nibbled her neck, while his rookers, now between her nogas, rubbed her until she began to spasm and jolt back and forth, trembling hard.

"Oh my gawd, look at this here!" said Mariel. While distracted just now, Kong turned over to Mariel, thus cutting short the time he spent with Yogita—but not with intention. The mood just seemed right with the timing. Boldly, while sensing that she definitely would want this, he lifted up Mariel's blouse sucking on her bra covered groodies. Her litso squinted and her glazzies clamped shut with passion. He took another step and unbuttoned her jeans. He touched her there, way down deep inside her panties.

"Oh fuck it!" Mariel began to shamelessly remove all her platties. As she was now lying on her back, Kong slid her narrow hips completely out of her red panties and nestled his gulliver between her nogas. Back and forth and side to side his yahzick performed over Mariel's clitoris. Mariel's nogas, extended in the air, were continuously jerking up and down.

"Ahhh, shit. I'M CUMMING! I'm cummin', cummin', ummin," Mariel panted and nearly passed out in front of her girls. She was really desperate for attention, but that was earlier. Now after all this, she felt even more shame.

"Okay! Now come on somebody gotta get fucked up in here!" Cecily said with wide glazzies.

There was silence in the room.

"Okay look, the Private VIP is on me. I am paying for it, so who is it going to be?" Cecily demanded.

No one volunteered.

"Look bitches don't make me waste my money, okay, please!" she added.

"Why don't she do it, she the one that brought Kong here?" Mariel insisted while pointing at Cecily.

"Go girl, you doing it, come on!" Brianna nudged Yogita in her side.

"Oh no I am not, I don't think so!" Yogita declared.

"This is Neteru Council!" Cecily quipped.

"We are all your sorority sisters here!" Brianna jumped in and the room immediately went into a death silence as everyone was staring at Yogita.

"You are safe with us!" Cecily assured Yogita.

"What do you mean I am safe with you?" Yogita asked.

"Here let me show you." Brianna goolied over and planted a wet hot kiss on the goobers of Yogita. Yogita never thought she was bisexual herself, but didn't seem to pull away from the action that was happening to her at this very moment with another woman. She was full on kissing Brianna. A strange tingle went through her plott as she felt others touching her as well. She was surrounded by many mirrors inside the booth. She thought of *The Zahyra Dangra* which meant *to be under a spell of sex* in the world of *Vodoun*. Indeed a spell was coming over her. She could feel weakness in her strength. *I must be drunk*. Yogita thought to herself. Suddenly everything went black.

CHAPTER 11

Lay everybody off?

Donovan McNabb lay on his bed, stripped to his boxers thinking on what the captain said about laying off some of the millicent force due to budget constraints. Could he be next to being out of a job? He always thought of why he had landed in this profession. Donovan sensed that the millicent was run by criminals who often got off the hook for planting false evidence on other people who already had a bad rap sheet and nobody to stand by their innocence. Most millicent staff feared the risk of getting killed if they spoke up against The Under Boss or "The Ministry of Interior" or more plainly the "Inside Job People." Nobody knew exactly just who The Under Boss truly was, but walls could talk, so you best follow the lead of everyone else. The pay was horrible. It only afforded him a single bedroom apartment in all of expensive Menap and Donovan was considering moving in with another roommate or sharing this apartment with someone, but he would have to install a rear okno. Bomb-shelter-roomed apartments were illegal in the city of Menap. In other words there was enough space in the rear of the apartment, except that it lacked a window to make it legal for him to rent. *Imagine this I am thirty-five springs and I still can't take care of myself.* Donovan cries to himself while laying down and staring up at the ceiling. His last roommate told him he was crazy and needed to seek professional mental help shortly before he confessed that he couldn't take anymore arguing and moved out. Back then this time around, the detective had saved up enough money to live alone while at that point he was living illegally in the space with an additional unauthorized tenant. The landlord didn't care as long as he got his rent in cash. But unfortunately, Donovan's savings was just about dwindling again. The other day he found rat dump around his apartment near the top of the stove. He can hear rats at night in the walls. Rats in Menap are huge. *Menap apartments look good on the outside, but they are shitty on the inside.* Donovan muttered this too himself and then he seeped deeper into his cries. He is constantly in heated arguments with the landlord about fixing stuff around the apartment. Last year the exterminators came in and rid the place of bed bugs, but now the place had rats and a fresh new colony of bed bugs.

Donovan McNabb is seemingly a forced bachelor economically, socially and emotionally. He is too hot-tempered to be in any relationship for too long. What woman would or should possibly want him? In his mind he is a failure that nobody understands. The last lady-friend that Donovan had over had spotted a few dead carcasses of several dead bed bugs near the pillowcases and she grabbed her purse and ran out for a cab which drove her off far away from his domy in a panic. He hasn't spoke to her since and that was several months ago. A talented guitarist, 15 years ago Donovan had once attempted being in a metal band while being a music student. The band was called *The Repukes* which was a derogatory spin off to mock The Republican Party from the old world.

Raised as the eldest of two boys by Irish-Pentecostal parents Donovan took after his uncle Prince Roger Nelson who played keyboard in a local jazz funk band called *The Democraps.* Prince would often explain to his young nephew that the inspiration of the name of the group came from an offensive address to The Democratic Party. As he would give lessons about music scales, Prince also gave important lessons to his nephew about how deceitful the government was all while expressing hate towards the millicent. The only way for Donovan to be free of it was to become a rockstar. But everyone just dismissed Prince as a fun loving hippy uncle that smoked too much weed. Donovan wanted to follow in his uncle's footsteps, but his parent's only approved of it as long as he took up a respectable major at school. So he chose to major in Psychology, but couldn't decide if he wanted to change his major to Journalism. Donovan loved to write short stories and as a young malchick he was always involved in afterschool youth writing programs. One of which he remembers was SCORES, an afterschool youth program that combined both poetry writing and soccer.

Just after completing his bachelors in Psychology, Donovan met up with some old band mates from The Repukes and decided to reform their group. But just as The Repukes had formed again, Donovan was soon asked to leave the band due to his extreme battle with stage fright.

The lead singer also felt that Donovan had anger issues in which resulted in being replaced by a more suitable lead guitarist.

"Maybe you need to get more in touch with your feminine side." Said Marc Bolan, the band's lead singer. But this didn't help much. Donovan was just afraid of being in front of people on stage. It never mattered that the group was a glam funk band in which men were required to wear eyeliner, feather boas and women's lace. It was just part of the act. Out of school and looking for work, Donovan had seen an advertisement to join the Menap Millicent Academy and has been with the Menap Millicent Department ever since, nine years total. Oddly enough he became exactly what his uncle would despise him to ever become—the police.

Not having much of a relationship with his parents— "the holy rollers"—a term he and his brother shared to describe their parent's religious fanaticism, Donovan sank further into his loneliness as the years had gone by. With no family and just a few friends Donovan stayed focused in his work a lot which required long hours both at the department and at the crime scenes. His younger brother escaped after being denied an exit visa and left Menap never to be seen or heard of again. He was feared to be killed by the hands of the guard patrol. Donovan failed to call his mother for her birthday and her twin felt that it was her duty to call her nephew to straighten out his selfish behavior. "Remember I washed and cleaned you and changed your dirty diapers. Don't forget that Donovan." His aunt said shortly before they ended the call. Whenever he could muster up the strength, Donovan would plug in his electric Fender Telecaster guitar and wobble away into the night singing while drinking a bottle of whiskey until he tired himself to sleep.

Last week things got really bad. Donovan had taken his revolver and put it to his temple in an attempt to *snuff it*. The suicide demon is something he has been grappling with more and more lately. Waking up in the middle of the night in a heated sweat was happening more often as well. Donovan had no one to turn to when he had these panic attacks. He loathed going to see a therapist for fear that they would tell him that he was indeed crazy. He was a loner and was embarrassed that he couldn't get his rassoodock in order. He couldn't sleep in the nochy and it was getting harder for him to obtain an appetite. One thing he couldn't stop thinking about was the rumor that the leader of the L-Comm gang put out a hit on several detectives lives. No one knew exactly on which detective this hit was put out for, but fear quickly spread throughout the department. A few detectives had reported being stalked and harassed, but they were mostly female detectives and sexual harassment on female employees was somewhat common both in and outside the department. The women were often blamed too by the government's establishment and feared losing their jobs if they spoke too soon about anything unusual. Most didn't govoreet although a few millicent women would show strength and make it a public issue that women were equal to men and not just sex objects. The millicent men on the other hand felt that harassment complaints compromised their masculinity and most withheld. But everyone knew of a grave new threat of millicent killers that was out there.

Overall, when it came to any particular threat against them, The Menap Millicent Department didn't just have the Italian mafia and the Quasi-Islamic gangs to deal with. They had an even deadlier gang on their hands. Both the Mara Salvatrucha and the Salvadorans With Pride were rivals at one another and known to be the deadliest gang members in all Menap. Flat out ruthless their members were getting younger and younger. Some were as young as eight years old when they first joined the gangs. Originating from the old world after seeking refuge from civil war in Central America, most of these gang members were born in America from a large wave of immigrants as a result to families fleeing an unstable environment in El Salvador.

In early 2004 a civil war erupted in El Salvador where estimates of about 300,000 people were killed by guns and also by machetes. Upwards of about three million undocumented El Salvadorans fled north from Central America over a course of five years and settled throughout many different states in the U.S. Some survivors of the massacre arrived missing a limb. Others had bullet wounds. Now up to this year 2089, the L-Comm population had tripled. The first large population of the L-Comm was settled in the lower districts of Manep. The area was already plagued with low-income members that settled there before and crime was at its all-time high. Now the newly arrived Central Americans were not as welcome and competition for meager jobs ensued riots between the newly arrived and the ones who were *here first*. A group of Salvadorans who wanted to separate themselves termed their newly appointed gang affiliation as Mara Salvatrucha—"La Mara"—which means in code "swarm of red ants." Trucha was slang for "beware" and also comes from being associated with the Salvadorian guerilla fighters. These guerilla fighters once referred to themselves as Salvatrucha when they joined an alliance with the Farabundo Marti National Front once a small labor activist group, but then formed into a larger political party as it was led by a well-respected and feared Central American guerilla fighter. The gang also is known as MS-13 where the letter M is the thirteen letter of the alphabet and also the letter M pays tribute to the Mexican Mafia.

The Menap Millicent Department feared that the same violent acts learned from El Salvador were being carried into Menap. The prison population inside the barry was overcrowded and simply couldn't house anymore inmates. Most of the prison's population was by gangs on death row with L-Comm gangs outnumbering the Asian-Veck, Anglo-Veck and Negro-Veck gangs all together. All prison populations were divided by race. It was simply too dangerous to house them all openly together, hate was too large in the inmates' hearts. Every once in a while a Negro-Veck inmate would get set-up by the correction officer called *operation slam.* Getting slammed in was an addictive blood sport that often took place wherever so often they would set the inmates up where one would get outnumbered by a group of hot-headed rivals. Say for instance a single Negro-Veck gang member would be thrown in with a bunch of L-Comm to get beaten to death. This was the same idea with a single L-Comm gang member getting thrown in with a bunch of Negro-Veck gang members to get beaten to death as well. This fueled even more hate throughout the barry. Oddly the L-Comm were more open to the idea of mixing with Anglo-Veck inmates to a certain degree, but never with another Negro-Veck. The Anglo-Veck inmates and Negro-Veck inmates couldn't even pass through the same area around meal time let alone live amongst each other. The results were often deadly. The Asian-Veck gangs were too small and less of a threat to anyone, but they still held a mild degree of power over themselves, but not much since they were always outnumbered by the others. They were viddied as a more neutral existing gang and usually stuck to themselves. There was an ongoing vicious rivalry between the Negro-Veck and L-Comm gangs over territory and respect both inside and outside the prison system. The Anglo-Veck gangs were just somehow caught in between.

What was worrisome to the bourgeoning elite of Menap was that gangs in general didn't seem scared of the establishment any longer. Getting locked up in the barry was seen as earning one's stripes to the gang and it didn't seem to deter any criminal activity. A gang leader could conduct business behind bars all the same. Life on the outside was getting tougher. Threats on the authoritative figure soared. Menap was undergoing a new era of lawlessness never seen before. High unemployment was to blame; steady at more than seventy-three percent, it had been at a crisis for more than forty years now in Menap.

FS "FUTURISTIC SPEECH" - GLOSSOPOEIA LANGUAGE CHART SHEET

FS	English
appy polly loggy	apology
baboochka	old woman
baddiwad	bad
banda	band
barry	prison
bezoomny	mad, crazy
biblio	library
bitva	battle
Bog	God
bolnoy	sick
bolshy	big, great
boohoo	to cry
brat, bratty	brother
bratchny	bastard
britva	razor

brooko	belly
brosay, brosat	to throw
bugatty	rich
cal	crap, shit
cancer	cigarette
cantora	office
carman	pocket
chai	tea
charles, charlie	chaplain
chasha	cup
chasso	guard
cheena	woman
cheest	to wash
chelloveck	person, man, fellow
chepooka	nonsense
choodessny	wonderful
chumble	to mumble
clop	to knock
cluve	beak
collocol	bell
crack	to break up, smash
crark	to howl
crast	steal, rob, robbery
creech	to shout, scream
cutter	money
dama	lady
ded, dedoochka	old man

deng	money
devotchka	young woman
dobby	good
dook	trace, ghost
domy	house
dorogoy	dear, valuable
dratsing	fighting
drencrom	drug
droog	friend
dung	to defecate
dva	two
eegra	game
eemya	name
eggiweg	egg
filly	to play or fool around with
firegold	drink
fist	to punch
flip	wild
forella	trout
fuzzy	scratchy
gazetta	newspaper
glazz, glazzies, glazzballs	eye, eyes (also used to refer to nipples)
gloopy	stupid
golly	unit of money
goloss	voice
goober	lip

gooly	to walk
gorlo	throat
govoreet	speak
grahzny	dirty
grazzy	soiled
gromky	loud
groody	breast
gruppa	group
gulliver	head
guttiwuts	guts
hen-korm	chickenfeed
horn	to cry out
horrorshow	good, well
in-out in-out, the old in and out	sexual intercourse/rape
interessovat	to interest
itty	to go
jammiwam	jam
jeezny	life
kartoffel	potatoes
kashl	cough
keeshkas	guts
kleb	bread
klootch	key
knives	drugs
knopka	button

kopat	to 'dig' (appreciate)
korova	cow
koshka, kot	cat, tomcat
koshtoom	clothing
krovvy	blood
kupet	to buy
lapa	paw
lewdies	people
litso	face
lomtick	piece, bit
luna	moon
loveted	caught
lubbilubbing	making love
luscious glory	hair
malchick	boy
malenky	little, tiny
maslo	butter
merzky	filthy
messel	thought, fancy
mesto	place
mewler (or: mowler)	to mew
millicents	police
minoota	minute
molodoy	young
moloko	milk

Moloko plus	<u>milk</u> laced with drugs, those being drencrom (which possibly refers to adrenochrome), synthemesc (which possibly refers to synthetic mescaline, mescaline being extracted from peyote, a mexican hallucinatory cactus used in rituals), or vellocet (-cet is a common ending for painkillers, and vello may refer to velocity, possibly referring to speed).
moodge	man
morder	snout
mounch	snack
mozg	brain
nachinat	to begin
nadmenny	arrogant
nadsat	teenage
nagoy	naked
nazz	fool
neezhnies	underpants
nochy	night
nogas	feet, legs
nozh	knife
nuking	smelling
oddy knocky	on one's own
odin	one
okno	window
oobivat	to kill
ookadeet	to leave

ooko	ear
oomny	brainy
oozhassny	terrible
oozy	chain
osoosh	to wipe
otchkies	eyeglasses
pan-handle	erection
pee and em	father and mother
peet	to drink
pishcha	food
platch	to cry
platties	clothes
pletcho	shoulder
plenny	prisoner
plesk	splash
plosh	to splash
plott	body
podooshka	pillow
pol	sex
polezny	useful
polyclef	skeleton key
pony	to understand
poogly	frightened
pooshka	gun
prestoopnik	criminal
privodeet	to lead somewhere
pretty polly	money
prod	to produce

ptitsa	girl
pyahnitsa	drunk

rabbit	work
radosty	joy
raskazz	story
rassoodock	mind
raz	time
razdraz	annoy
razrez	to rip, ripping
rookers	arms, hands
rot	mouth
rozz	policeman

sabog	shoe
sakar	sugar
sammy	generous
scoteena	beast
shaika	gang
sharp	female
sharries	buttocks
shest	barrier
shilarny	concern
shive	slice
shiyah	neck
shlem	helmet
shlaga	club
shlapa	hat
shoom	noise

shoot	fool
sinny	cinema
skazat	to say
skolliwoll	school
skorry	quick, quickly
skriking	scratching
skvat	to grab
sladky	sweet
sloochat	to happen
sloosh, slooshy	to hear, to listen
slovo(s)	word(s)
smeck	laugh
smot	to look
sneety	dream
snoutie	tobacco
snuff it	commit suicide
sobirat	to pick up
sod	to fornicate, fornicator
soomka	old woman
sooka	whore
soviet	advice, order
spat, spatchka	to sleep
splodge, splosh	splash
spoogy	terrified
Staja	cell, State Jail
starry	ancient, old
strack	horror
synthemesc	drug

tally	waist
tashtook	handkerchief
tass	cup
tick-tocker	heart
timps	drums
tolchock	push, hit
toofles	slippers
tree	three

vareet	to cook up
vaysay	washroom
veck	(see chelloveck)
vehina	wine
vellocet	drug
venail	(used as tolchocking and venailing)
veshch	thing
viddy	see
vino	wine (also used as blood)
voloss	hair
von	smell
vred	to harm or damage

warbles	songs

yahma	hole
yahoodies	Jews
yahzick	tongue
yarbles, yarblockos	testicles
yeckate	to drive

zammechat	remarkable
zasnoot	sleep
zheena	wife
zoobies	teeth
zvonock	bellpull
zvook	sound

Printed in the United States
by Baker & Taylor Publisher Services